THE HOUSE OF STRANGE STORIES

Ruskin Bond is known for his signature simplistic and witty writing style. He is the author of several bestselling short stories, novellas, collections, essays and children's books; and has contributed a number of poems and articles to various magazines and anthologies. At the age of twenty-three, he won the prestigious John Llewellyn Rhys Prize for his first novel, *The Room on the Roof*. He was also the recipient of the Padma Shri in 1999, Lifetime Achievement Award by the Delhi Government in 2012, and the Padma Bhushan in 2014.

Born in 1934, Ruskin Bond grew up in Jamnagar, Shimla, New Delhi and Dehradun. Apart from three years in the UK, he has spent all his life in India, and now lives in Landour, Mussoorie, with his adopted family.

THE HOUSE OF STRANGE STORIES

Selected and Compiled by
RUSKIN BOND

Published by
Rupa Publications India Pvt. Ltd 2018
7/16, Ansari Road, Daryaganj
New Delhi 110002

Sales centres:
Prayagraj Bengaluru Chennai
Hyderabad Jaipur Kathmandu
Kolkata Mumbai

Copyright © Ruskin Bond 2018

This is a work of fiction. Names, characters, places and incidents are either the product of the author's imagination or are used fictitiously and any resemblance to any actual person, living or dead, events or locales is entirely coincidental.

All rights reserved.
No part of this publication may be reproduced, transmitted, or stored in a retrieval system, in any form or by any means, electronic, mechanical, photocopying, recording or otherwise, without the prior permission of the publisher.

ISBN: 978-93-530-4353-7

Twentieth impression 2023

25 24 23 22 21 20

Printed in India

This book is sold subject to the condition that it shall not, by way of trade or otherwise, be lent, resold, hired out, or otherwise circulated, without the publisher's prior consent, in any form of binding or cover other than that in which it is published.

CONTENTS

Introduction — vii

The House of Strange Stories — 1
  Andrew Lang
From the Primaeval Past — 11
Some Hill Station Ghosts — 15
Pret in the House — 23
A Traveller's Tale — 28
The Chakrata Cat — 34
A Dreadful Gurgle — 38
The White Pigeon — 41
He Who Rides a Tiger — 43
The Wind on Haunted Hill — 46
A Job Well Done — 52
A Face Under the Pillow — 58
A Demon for Work — 61
The Overcoat — 65
Eyes of the Cat — 69

The Perfect Murder *Stacy Aumonier*	72
The Red-Headed League *Arthur Conan Doyle*	93
The Lodger *Marie Belloc Lowndes*	125
The Duel *Wilkie Collins*	163
The Cask of Amontillado *Edgar Allan Poe*	180
The Squaw *Bram Stoker*	189

INTRODUCTION

Strange does not always necessarily mean horror. Claustrophobic settings and threatening situations can make for just as grisly tales that do not disappoint horror addicts. I think that it is the difference between the real and the imaginary which makes for strange territory.

A group of friends sitting together at night and sharing their eerie, unnatural experiences, as in Andrew Lang's 'The House of Strange Stories' can be quite a sinister experience. Two French brothers planning a murder within the family that ends up going horribly wrong, as in Stacy Aumonier's 'The Perfect Murder', can make any reader go edgy. A reclusive lodger's arrival coinciding with serial murders taking place in the city of London, in Marie Belloc Lowndes' 'The Lodger' is as disturbing as it gets. No wonder Alfred Hitchcock's very first suspense film was based on this story. It has in fact been filmed several times. When Sherlock Holmes gets involved in a mystery, rest assured you know you are in for an unbeatable treat, as you will find out in 'The Red-Headed League'.

Accompanying these tales are a few of my own—where I talk about Chakrata's infamous cat feared for its vampire-like qualities; a ghost that took refuge in my grandfather's house;

a giant succubus that would rise from a pond near Rajpur and would envelope any human around; the ghost of the long-dead Julie who borrowed my overcoat one winter evening; and many more in my macabre vein!

I would suggest you pick a full moon night, and when the moonlight streams in through your window…switch on dim lights and get ready to read these strange, very strange stories.

Ruskin Bond

THE HOUSE OF STRANGE STORIES
Andrew Lang

The House of Strange Stories, as I prefer to call it (though it is not known by that name in the country), seems the very place for a ghost. Yet, though so many people have dwelt upon its site and in its chambers, though the ancient Elizabethan oak, and all the queer tables and chairs that a dozen generations have bequeathed, might well be tenanted by ancestral spirits, and disturbed by rappings, it is a curious fact that there is *not* a ghost in the House of Strange Stories. On my earliest visit to this mansion, I was disturbed, I own, by a not unpleasing expectancy. There *must*, one argued, be a shadowy lady in green in the bedroom, or, just as one was falling asleep, the spectre of a Jesuit would creep out of the priest's hole, where he was starved to death in the 'spacious times of great Elizabeth,' and would search for a morsel of bread.

'Does the priest of your "priest-hole" walk?' I asked the squire one winter evening in the House of Strange Stories.

Darkness had come to the rescue of the pheasants at about four in the afternoon, and all of us, men and women, were sitting at afternoon tea in the firelit study, drowsily watching the flicker of the flames on the black panelling. The characters will introduce themselves, as they take part in the conversation.

'No,' said the squire, 'even the priest does not walk. Somehow very few of the Jesuits have left ghosts in country houses. They are just the customers you would expect to "walk", but they don't...'

'The only ghost *I* ever came across, or, rather, came within measurable distance of, never appeared at all so far as one knew,' remarked the Girton girl.

'Miss Lebas has a story,' said the squire, 'Won't she tell us her story?'

The ladies murmured, 'Do, please.'

'It really cannot be called a ghost-story,' remarked Miss Lebas, 'it was only an uncomfortable kind of coincidence, and I never think of it without a shudder. But I know there is not any reason at all why it should make any of you shudder; so don't be disappointed.

'It was the long vacation before last, and I went on a reading party to Bantry Bay. Term-time was drawing near, and Bantry Bay was getting pretty cold, when I received an invitation from Lady Garryowen to stay with them at Dundellan on my way south. They were two very dear, old, hospitable Irish ladies, the last of their race, Lady Garryowen and her sister, Miss Patty. They were *so* hospitable that, though I did not know it, Dundellan was quite full when I reached it, overflowing with young people. The house has nothing very remarkable about it: a grey, plain building, with remains of the chateau about it, and a high park wall. In the garden wall there is a small round tower, just like those in the precinct wall at St Andrews. The ground floor is not used. On the first floor there is a furnished chamber with a deep round niche, almost a separate room, like that in Queen Mary's apartments in Holy Rood. The first floor has long been fitted up as a bedroom and dressing-room, but it had not been occupied, and a curious old spinning-wheel in the corner (which has nothing to do with my story, if you can call it a story), must have been unused since 1798, at least. I reached Dublin late; our train should have arrived at half-past six—it was ten before we toiled into the station. The Dundellan carriage was waiting for me, and, after an hour's drive, I reached the house. The dear old ladies had sat up for me, and I went to bed as soon as possible in a very comfortable room. I fell asleep at once, and did not waken until broad daylight, between seven and eight, when, as my eyes wandered about, I saw, by the pictures on the wall, and the names on the books beside my bed, that Miss Patty must have given up her own room to me. I was quite sorry and, as I dressed, determined to get her to let me change into any den rather than accept this sacrifice. I went downstairs, and found breakfast ready, but neither Lady Garryowen nor Miss Patty. Looking out of the window into the garden, I heard, for the only time in my life, the wild Irish *keen* over the dead, and saw the old nurse wailing and wringing her hands and hurrying to the house. As soon as she entered she told me, with a burst of grief, and in a language I shall not try to imitate, that Miss Patty was dead.

'When I arrived the house was so full that there was literally no room for me. But "Dundellan was never beaten yet", the old ladies had said. There was still the room in the tower. But this room had such an evil reputation for being "haunted" that the servants could hardly be got to go near it, at least after dark, and the dear old ladies never dreamed of sending any of their guests to pass a bad night in a place with a bad name. Miss Patty, who had the courage of a Bayard, did not think twice. She went herself to sleep in the haunted tower, and left her room to me. And when the old nurse went to call her in the morning, she could not waken Miss Patty. She was dead. Heart-disease, they called it. Of course,' added the Girton girl, 'as I said, it was only a coincidence. But the Irish servants could not be persuaded that Miss Patty had not seen whatever the thing was that they believed to be in the garden tower. I don't know what it was. You see the context was dreadfully vague, a mere fragment.'

There was a little silence after the Girton girl's story.

'I never heard before in my life,' said the maiden aunt, at last, 'of any host or hostess who took the haunted room themselves, when the house happened to be full. They always send the stranger within their gates to it, and then pretend to be vastly surprised when he does not have a good night. I had several bad nights myself once. In Ireland too.'

'Tell us all about it, Judy,' said her brother, the squire.

'No,' murmured the maiden aunt. 'You would only laugh at me. There was no ghost. I didn't hear anything. I didn't see anything. I didn't even *smell* anything, as they do in that horrid book, *The Haunted Hotel*.'

'Then why had you such bad nights?'

'Oh, I *felt*,' said the maiden aunt, with a little shudder.

'What did you feel, Aunt Judy?'

'I *know* you will laugh,' said the maiden aunt, abruptly entering on her nervous narrative. 'I felt all the time *as if somebody was looking through the window.* Now, you know, there *couldn't* be anybody. It was in an Irish country house where I had just arrived, and my room was on the second floor. The window was old-fashioned and narrow, with a deep recess. As soon as I went to bed, my dears, I *felt* that someone was looking through the window, and meant to come in. I got up, and bolted the window, though I knew it was impossible for anybody to climb up there, and I drew the curtains, but I could not fall asleep. If ever I began to doze, I would waken with a start, and turn and look in the direction of the window. I did not sleep all night, and the next night, though I was dreadfully tired, it was just the same thing. So I had to take my hostess into my confidence, though it was extremely disagreeable, my dears, to seem so foolish. I only told her that I thought the air, or something, must disagree with me, for I could not sleep. Then, as someone was leaving the house that day, she implored me to try another room, where I slept beautifully, and afterwards had a very pleasant visit. But, the day I went away, my hostess asked me if I had been kept awake by anything in particular, for instance, by a feeling that someone was trying to come in at the window. Well, I admitted that I had a nervous feeling of that sort, and she said that she was very sorry, and that everyone who lay in the room had exactly the same sensation. She supposed they must all have heard the history of the room, in childhood, and forgotten that they had heard it, and then been unconsciously reminded of it by reflex action. It seems, my dears, that that is the new scientific way of explaining all these things, presentiments and dreams and wraiths, and all that sort of thing. We have seen them before, and remember them without being aware of it. So I said I'd never heard the history of the room; but she said I *must* have, and so must all the people who felt as if someone was coming in by the window. And I said that it was rather a curious thing they should *all* forget they knew it, and *all* be reminded of it without being aware of it, and that, if she did not mind, I'd like to be reminded of it again. So she said that these objections had all been replied to (just as clergymen always say in sermons), and then she told me the history of the room. It only came to this that three generations before, the family butler (whom everyone had always thought a most steady, respectable man), dressed himself up like a ghost, or like his notion of a ghost, and got a ladder, and came in by the window to steal the diamonds of the lady of the house, and he frightened her to death, poor woman! That was all. But, ever since, people who sleep in the room don't sleep, so to speak, and keep thinking that someone is coming in by the casement. That's all; and I told you it was not an interesting story, but perhaps you will find more interest in the scientific explanation of all these things.'

The story of the maiden aunt, so far as it recounted her own experience, did not contain anything to which the judicial faculties of the mind refused assent. Probably the Bachelor of Arts felt that something a good deal more unusual was wanted, for he instantly started, without being asked, on the following narrative:

'I also was staying,' said the Bachelor of Arts, 'at the home of my friends, the aristocracy in Scotland. The name of the house, and the precise rank in the peerage of my illustrious host, it is not necessary for me to give. All those, however, who know of feudal and baronial halls are aware that the front of the castle looks forth on a somewhat narrow drive, bordered by black and funereal pines. On the night of my arrival at the castle, although I went late to bed, I did not feel at all sleepy. Something, perhaps, in the mountain air, or in the vicissitudes of *baccarat*, may have banished slumber. I had been in luck, and a pile of sovereigns and notes lay, in agreeable confusion, on my dressing table. My feverish blood declined to be tranquillized, and at last I drew up the blind, threw open the latticed window, and looked out on the drive and the pine-wood. The faint and silvery blue of dawn was just wakening in the sky, and a setting moon hung, with a peculiarly ominous and wasted appearance, above the crests of the forest. But conceive my astonishment when I beheld, on the drive, and right under my window, a large and well-appointed hearse, with two white horses, with plumes complete and attended by mutes, whose black staffs were tipped with silver that glittered pallid in the dawn.

'I exhausted my ingenuity in conjectures as to the presence of this remarkable vehicle with the white horses, so unusual, though, when one thinks of it, so appropriate to the chariot of Death. Could some belated visitor have arrived in a hearse, like the lady in Miss Ferrier's novel? Could one of the domestics have expired, and was it the intention of my host to have the body thus honourably removed without casting a gloom over his guests?

'Wild as these hypotheses appeared, I could think of nothing better, and was just about to leave the window, and retire to bed, when the driver of the strange carriage, who had hitherto sat motionless, turned, and looked me full in the face. Never shall I forget the appearance of this man, whose sallow countenance, close-shaven dark skin, and a small, black moustache, combined with I know not what of martial in his air, struck into me a certain indefinable alarm. No sooner had he caught my eye than he gathered up his reins, raised his whip, and started the mortuary vehicle at a walk down the road. I followed it with my eyes until a bend in the avenue hid it from my sight. So wrapt up was my spirit in the exercise of the single sense of vision that it was not until the hearse became lost to view that I noticed the entire absence of sound which accompanied its departure. Neither had the bridles and trappings of the white horses jingled as the animals shook their heads, nor had the wheels of the hearse crashed upon the gravel of the avenue. I was compelled by all these circumstances to believe that what I had looked upon was not of this world, and, with a beating heart, I sought refuge in sleep.

'Next morning, feeling far from refreshed, I arrived among the latest at a breakfast which was a desultory and movable feast. Almost all the men had gone forth to hill, forest, or river, in pursuit of the furred, finned, or feathered denizens of the wilds—'

'You speak,' interrupted the schoolboy, 'like a printed book! I like to hear you speak like that. Drive on, old man! Drive on your hearse!'

The Bachelor of Arts 'drove on', without noticing this interruption. 'I tried to "lead up" to the hearse,' he said, 'in conversation with the young ladies of the castle. I endeavoured to assume the languid and preoccupied air of the guest who, in ghost-stories, has had a bad night with the family spectre. I drew the conversation to the topic of apparitions, and even warnings of death. I knew that every family worthy of the name has its omen: the Oxenhams a white bird, another house a brass band, whose airy music in poured forth by invisible performers, and so on. Of course I expected someone to cry, "Oh, *we've* got a hearse with white horses," for that is the kind of heirloom an ancient house regards with complacent pride. But nobody offered any remarks on the local omen, and even when I drew near the topic of *hearses*, one of the girls, my cousin, merely quoted, "Speak not like a death's-head, good Doll" (my name is Adolphus), and asked me to play lawn-tennis.'

'In the evening, in the smoking-room, it was no better, nobody had ever heard of an omen in this particular castle. Nay, when I told my story, for it came to that at last, they only laughed at me, and said I must have dreamed it. Of course I expected to be wakened in the night by some awful apparition, but nothing disturbed me. I never slept better, and hearses were the last things I thought of during the remainder of my visit. Months passed, and I had almost forgotten the vision, or dream, for I began to feel apprehensive that, after all, it *was* a dream. So costly and elaborate an apparition as a hearse, with white horses and plumes complete, could never have been got up, regardless of expense, for one occasion only, and to frighten one undergraduate, yet it was certain that the hearse was not "the old family coach". My entertainers had undeniably never heard of it in their lives before. Even tradition at the castle said nothing of a spectral hearse, though the house was credited with a white lady deprived of her hands, and a luminous boy.'

Here the Bachelor of Arts paused, and a shower of chaff began.

'Is that really all?' asked the Girton girl. 'Why, this is the third ghost-story tonight without any ghost in it!'

'I don't remember saying that it *was* a ghost-story,' replied the Bachelor of Arts; 'but I thought a little anecdote of a mere "warning" might not be unwelcome.'

'But where does the warning come in?' asked the schoolboy.

'That's just what I was arriving at,' replied the narrator, 'when I was interrupted with as little ceremony as if I had been Mr Gladstone in the middle of a most important speech. I was going to say that, in the Easter vacation after my visit to the castle, I went over to Paris with a friend, a fellow of my college. We drove to the *Hôtel d' Alsace* (I believe there is no hotel of that name; if there is, I beg the spirited proprietor's pardon, and assure him that nothing personal is intended). We marched upstairs with our bag and baggage, and jolly high stairs they were. When we had removed the soil of travel from our persons, my friend called out to me, "I say, Jones, why shouldn't we go down by the lift?" "All right," said I, and my friend walked to the door of the mechanical apparatus, opened it, and got in. I followed him, when the porter whose business it is to "personally conduct" the inmates of the hotel, entered also, and was closing the door.

'His eyes met mine, and I knew him in a moment. I had seen him once before. His sallow face, black, closely shaven chin, furtive glance, and military bearing, were the face and the glance and bearing of the driver of that awful hearse!

'In a moment—more swiftly than I can tell you—I pushed past the man, threw open the door, and just managed, by a violent effort, to drag my friend on to the landing. Then the lift rose with a sudden impulse, fell again, and rushed, with frightful velocity, to the basement of the hotel, whence we heard an appalling crash, followed by groans. We rushed downstairs, and the horrible spectacle of destruction that met our eyes I shall never forget. The unhappy porter was expiring in agony; but the warning had saved my life and my friend's.'

'*I was that friend*, said I—the collector of these anecdotes; 'and so far I can testify to the truth of Jones's story.'

At this moment, however, the gong for dressing sounded, and we went to our several apartments, after this emotional specimen of 'Evenings at Home'.

FROM THE PRIMAEVAL PAST

I discovered the pool near Rajpur on a hot summer's day, some fifteen years ago. It was shaded by close-growing sal trees, and looked cool and inviting. I took off my clothes and dived in.

The water was colder than I had expected. It was icy, glacial cold. The sun never touched it for long, I supposed. Striking out vigorously, I swam to the other end of the pool and pulled myself up on the rocks, shivering.

But I wanted to swim. So I dived in again and did a gentle breast-stroke towards the middle of the pool. Something slid between my legs. Something slimy, pulpy. I could see no one, hear nothing. I swam away, but the floating, slippery thing followed me. I did not like it. Something curled around my leg. Not an underwater plant. Something that sucked at my foot. A long tongue licking at my calf. I struck out wildly, thrust myself away from whatever it was that sought my company. Something lonely, lurking in the shadows. Kicking up spray, I swam like a frightened porpoise fleeing from some terror of the deep.

Safely out of the water, I looked for a warm, sunny rock, and stood there looking down at the water.

Nothing stirred. The surface of the pool was now calm and undisturbed. Just a few fallen leaves floating around. Not a frog, not a fish, not a water-bird in sight. And that in itself seemed strange, for you would have expected some sort of pond life to have been in evidence.

But something lived in the pool, of that I was sure. Something very cold-blooded; colder and wetter than the water. Could it have been a corpse trapped in the weeds? I did not want to know; so I dressed and hurried away.

A few days later I left for Delhi, where I went to work in an ad agency, telling people how to beat the summer heat by drinking fizzy drinks that made you thirstier. The pool in the forest was forgotten. And it was ten years before I visited Rajpur again.

Leaving the small hotel where I was staying, I found myself walking through the same old sal forest, drawn almost irresistibly towards the pool where I had not been able to finish my swim. I was not over-eager to swim there again, but I was curious to know if the pool still existed.

Well, it was there all right, although the surroundings had changed and a number of new houses and buildings had come up where formerly there had only been wilderness. And there was a fair amount of activity in the vicinity of the pool.

A number of labourers were busy with buckets and rubber pipes, doing their best to empty the pool. They had also dammed off and diverted the little stream that fed it.

Overseeing this operation was a well-dressed man in a white safari suit. I thought at first that he was an honorary forest warden, but it turned out that he was the owner of a new school that had come up nearby.

'Do you live in Rajpur?' he asked. 'I used to…once upon a time…Why are you draining the pool?'

'It's become a hazard,' he said. 'Two of my boys were

drowned here recently. Both senior students. Of course they weren't supposed to be swimming here without permission, the pool is off limits. But you know what boys are like. Make a rule and they feel duty-bound to break it.'

He told me his name, Kapoor, and led me back to his house, a newly-built bungalow with a wide cool verandah. His servant brought us glasses of cool sherbet. We sat in cane chairs overlooking the pool and the forest. Across a clearing, a gravelled road led to the school buildings, newly white-washed and glistening in the sun.

'Were the boys there at the same time?' I asked.

'Yes, they were friends. And they must have been attacked by fiends. Limbs twisted and broken, faces disfigured. But death was due to drowning—that was the verdict of the medical examiner.'

We gazed down at the shallows of the pool, where a couple of men were still at work, the others having gone for their mid-day meal.

'Perhaps it would be better to leave the place alone,' I said. 'Put a barbed-wire fence around it. Keep your boys away. Thousands of years ago this valley was an inland sea. A few small pools and streams are all that is left of it.'

'I want to fill it in and build something there. An open-air theatre, maybe. We can always create an artificial pond somewhere else.'

Presently only one man remained at the pool, knee-deep in muddy, churned-up water. And Mr Kapoor and I both saw what happened next.

Something rose out of the bottom of the pool. It looked like a giant snail, but its head was part human, its body and limbs part squid or octopus. An enormous succubus. It stood taller than the man in the pool. A creature soft and slimy, a survivor from our primaeval past.

With a great sucking motion it enveloped the man completely, so that only his arms and legs could be seen thrashing about wildly and futilely. The succubus dragged him down under the water.

Kapoor and I left the verandah and ran to the edge of the pool. Bubbles rose from the green scum near the surface. All was still and silent. And then, like bubble-gum issuing from the mouth of a child, the mangled body of the man shot out of the water and came spinning towards us.

Dead and drowned and sucked dry of its fluids.

Naturally no more work was done at the pool. A labourer had slipped and fallen to his death on the rocks, that was the story that was put out. Kapoor swore me to secrecy. His school would have to close down if there were too many strange drownings and accidents in its vicinity. But he walled the place off from his property and made it practically inaccessible. The jungle's undergrowth now hides the approach.

The monsoon rains came and the pool filled up again. I can tell you how to get there, if you'd like to see it. But I wouldn't advise you to go for a swim.

SOME HILL STATION GHOSTS

Shimla has its phantom-rickshaw and Lansdowne its headless horseman. Mussoorie has its woman in white. Late at night, she can be seen sitting on the parapet wall on the winding road up to the hill station. Don't stop to offer her a lift. She will fix you with her evil eye and ruin your holiday.

The Mussoorie taxi drivers and other locals call her Bhoot Aunty. Everyone has seen her at some time or the other. To give her a lift is to court disaster. Many accidents have been attributed to her baleful presence. And when people pick themselves up from the road (or are picked up by concerned citizens), Bhoot Aunty is nowhere to be seen, although survivors swear that she was in the car with them.

Ganesh Saili, Abha and I were coming back from Dehradun late one night when we saw this woman in white sitting on the parapet by the side of the road. As our headlights fell on her, she turned her face away, Ganesh, being a thorough gentleman, slowed down and offered her a lift. She turned towards us then, and smiled a wicked smile. She seemed quite attractive except that her canines protruded slightly in vampire fashion.

'Don't stop!' screamed Abha. 'Don't even look at her! It's Aunty!'

Ganesh pressed down on the accelerator and sped past her. Next day we heard that a tourist's car had gone off the road and the occupants had been severely injured. The accident took place shortly after they had stopped to pick up a woman in white who had wanted a lift. But she was not among the injured.

◆

Miss Ripley-Bean, an old English lady who was my neighbour when I lived near Wynberg-Allen school, told me that her family was haunted by a malignant phantom head that always appeared before the death of one of her relatives.

She said her brother saw this apparition the night before her mother died, and both she and her sister saw it before the death of their father. The sister slept in the same room. They were both awakened one night by a curious noise in the cupboard facing their beds. One of them began getting out of bed to see if their cat was in the room, when the cupboard door suddenly opened and a luminous head appeared. It was covered with matted hair and appeared to be in an advanced stage of decomposition. Its fleshless mouth grinned at the terrified sisters. And then as they crossed themselves, it vanished. The next day they learned that their father, who was in Lucknow, had died suddenly, at about the time that they had seen the death's head.

◆

Everyone likes to hear stories about haunted houses; even sceptics will listen to a ghost story, while casting doubts on its veracity.

Rudyard Kipling wrote a number of memorable ghost stories set in India—*Imray's Return, The Phantom 'Rickshaw, The Mark of the Beast, The End of the Passage*—his favourite milieu being the haunted dak bungalow. But it was only after his return to England that he found himself actually having to live in a haunted house. He writes about it in his autobiography, *Something of Myself.*

The spring of '96 saw us in Torquay, where we found a house for our heads that seemed almost too good to be true. It was large and bright, with big rooms each and all open to the sun, the ground embellished with great trees and the warm land dipping southerly to the clean sea under the Mary Church cliffs. It had been inhabited for thirty years by three old maids.

The revelation came in the shape of a growing depression which enveloped us both—a gathering blackness of mind and sorrow of the heart, that each put down to the new, soft climate and, without telling the other, fought against for long weeks. It was the Feng-shui—the spirit of the house itself—that darkened the sunshine and fell upon us every time we entered, checking the very words on our lips... We paid forfeit and fled. More than thirty years later we returned down the steep little road to that house, and found, quite unchanged, the same brooding spirit of deep despondency within the rooms.

Again, thirty years later, he returned to this house in his short story, 'The House Surgeon', in which two sisters cannot come to terms with the suicide of a third sister, and brood upon the tragedy day and night until their thoughts saturate every room of the house.

Many years ago, I had a similar experience in a house in Dehradun, in which an elderly English couple had died from neglect and starvation. In 1947, when many European residents were leaving the town and emigrating to the UK, this poverty-stricken old couple, sick and friendless, had been forgotten. Too ill to go out for food or medicine, they had died in their beds, where they were discovered several days later by the landlord's munshi.

The house stood empty for several years. No one wanted to live in it. As a young man, I would sometimes roam about the neglected grounds or explore the cold, bare rooms, now stripped of furniture, doorless and windowless, and I would be assailed by a feeling of deep gloom and depression. Of course I knew what had happened there, and that may have contributed to the effect the place had on me. But when I took a friend, Jai Shankar, through the house, he told me he felt quite sick with apprehension and fear. 'Ruskin, why have you brought me to this awful house?' he said. 'I'm sure it's haunted.' And only then did I tell him about the tragedy that had taken place within its walls.

Today, the house is used as a government office. No one lives in it at night except for a Gurkha chowkidar, a man of strong nerves who sleeps in the back verandah. The atmosphere of the place doesn't bother him, but he does hear strange sounds in the night. 'Like someone crawling about on the floor above,' he tells me. 'And someone groaning. These old houses are noisy places...'

◆

A morgue is not a noisy place, as a rule. And for a morgue attendant, corpses are silent companions.

Old Mr Jacob, who lives just behind the cottage, was once a morgue attendant for the local mission hospital. In those days it was situated at Sunny Bank, about a hundred metres up the hill from here. One of the outhouses served as the morgue: Mr Jacob begs me not to identify it.

He tells me of a terrifying experience he went through

when he was doing night duty at the morgue.

'The body of a young man was found floating in the Aglar River, behind Landour, and was brought to the morgue while I was on night duty. It was placed on the table and covered with a sheet.

'I was quite accustomed to seeing corpses of various kinds and did not mind sharing the same room with them, even after dark. On this occasion a friend had promised to join me, and to pass the time I strolled around the room, whistling a popular tune. I think it was 'Danny Boy', if I remember right. My friend was a long time coming, and I soon got tired of whistling and sat down on the bench beside the table. The night was very still, and I began to feel uneasy. My thoughts went to the boy who had drowned and I wondered what he had been like when he was alive. Dead bodies are so impersonal...

'The morgue had no electricity, just a kerosene lamp, and after some time I noticed that the flame was very low. As I was about to turn it up, it suddenly went out. I lit the lamp again, after extending the wick. I returned to the bench, but I had not been sitting there for long when the lamp again went out, and something moved very softly and quietly past me.

'I felt quite sick and faint, and could hear my heart pounding away. The strength had gone out of my legs, otherwise I would have fled the room. I felt quite weak and helpless, unable even to call out.

'Presently the footsteps came nearer and nearer. Something cold and icy touched one of my hands and felt its way up towards my neck and throat. It was behind me, then it was before me. Then it was *over* me. I was in the arms of the corpse!

'I must have fainted, because when I woke up I was on the floor, and my friend was trying to revive me. The corpse was back on the table.'

'It may have been a nightmare,' I suggested. 'Or you allowed your imagination to run riot.'

'No,' said Mr Jacobs. 'There were wet, slimy marks on my clothes. And the feet of the corpse matched the wet footprints on the floor.'

After this experience, Mr Jacobs refused to do any more night duty at the morgue.

◆

From Herbertpur near Paonta you can go up to Kalsi, and then up the hill road to Chakrata.

Chakrata is in a security zone, most of it off limits to tourists, which is one reason why it has remained unchanged in 150 years of its existence. This small town's population of 1,500 is the same today as it was in 1947—probably the only town in India that hasn't shown a population increase.

Courtesy a government official, I was fortunate enough to be able to stay in the forest rest house on the outskirts of the town. This is a new building, the old rest house—a little way downhill—having fallen into disuse. The chowkidar told me the old rest house was haunted, and that this was the real reason for its having been abandoned. I was a bit sceptical about this, and asked him what kind of haunting took place in it. He told me that he had himself gone through a frightening experience in the old house, when he had gone there to light a fire for some forest officers who were expected that night. After lighting the fire, he looked round and saw a large black animal, like a wild cat, sitting on the wooden floor and gazing into the fire. 'I called out to it, thinking it was someone's pet. The creature turned, and looked full at me with eyes that were human, and a face which was the face of an ugly woman. The creature snarled at me, and the snarl became an angry howl. Then it vanished!'

'And what did you do?' I asked.

'I vanished too,' said the chowkidar. I haven't been down to that house again.'

I did not volunteer to sleep in the old house but made myself comfortable in the new one, where I hoped I would not be troubled by any phantom. However, a large rat kept me company, gnawing away at the woodwork of a chest of drawers. Whenever I switched on the light it would be silent, but as soon as the light was off, it would start gnawing away again.

This reminded me of a story old Miss Kellner (of my Dehra childhood) told me, of a young man who was desperately in love with a girl who did not care for him. One day, when he was following her in the street, she turned on him and, pointing to a rat which some boys had just killed, said, 'I'd as soon marry that rat as marry you.' He took her cruel words so much to heart that he pined away and died. After his death the girl was haunted at night by a rat and occasionally she would be bitten. When the family decided to emigrate, they travelled down to Bombay in order to embark on a ship sailing for London. The ship had just left the quay, when shouts and screams were heard from the pier. The crowd scattered, and a huge rat with fiery eyes ran down to the end of the quay. It sat there, screaming with rage, then jumped into the water and disappeared. After that (according to Miss Kellner), the girl was not haunted again.

Old dak bungalows and forest rest houses have a reputation for being haunted. And most hill stations have their resident ghosts—and ghost writers! But I will not extend this catalogue of ghostly hauntings and visitations, as I do not want to discourage tourists from visiting Landour and Mussoorie. In some countries, ghosts are an added attraction for tourists. Britain boasts of hundreds of haunted castles and stately homes, and visitors to Romania seek out Transylvania and Dracula's castle. So do we promote Bhoot Aunty as a tourist attraction? Only if she reforms and stops sending vehicles off those hairpin bends that lead to Mussoorie.

PRET IN THE HOUSE

It was Grandmother who decided that we must move to another house. And it was all because of a pret, a mischievous ghost, who had been making life intolerable for everyone.

In India, prets usually live in peepul trees, and that's where our pret first had his abode—in the branches of an old peepul which had grown through the compound wall and had spread into the garden, on our side, and over the road, on the other side.

For many years, the pret had lived there quite happily, without bothering anyone in the house. I suppose the traffic on the road had kept him fully occupied. Sometimes, when a tonga was passing, he would frighten the pony and, as a result, the little pony-cart would go reeling off the road. Occasionally he would get into the engine of a car or bus, which would soon afterwards have a breakdown. And he liked to knock the sola-topis off the heads of Sahibs, who would curse and wonder how a breeze had sprung up so suddenly, only to die down again just as quickly. Although the pret could make himself felt, and sometimes heard, he was invisible to the human eye.

At night, people avoided walking beneath the peepul tree. It was said that if you yawned beneath the tree, the pret would jump down your throat and ruin your digestion. Grandmother's tailor, Jaspal, who never had anything ready on time, blamed the pret for all his troubles. Once, when yawning, Jaspal had forgotten to snap his fingers in front of his mouth—always mandatory when yawning beneath peepul trees—and the pret had got in without any difficulty. Since then, Jaspal had always been suffering from tummy upsets.

But it had left our family alone until, one day, the peepul tree had been cut down.

It was nobody's fault except, of course, that Grandfather had given the Public Works Department permission to cut the tree which had been standing on our land. They wanted to widen the road, and the tree and a bit of wall were in the way; so both had to go. In any case, not even a ghost can prevail against the PWD. But hardly a day had passed when we discovered that the pret, deprived of his tree, had decided to take up residence in the bungalow. And since a good pret must be bad in order to justify his existence, he was soon up to all sorts of mischief in the house.

He began by hiding Grandmother's spectacles whenever she took them off.

'I'm sure I put them down on the dressing-table,' she grumbled.

A little later they were found balanced precariously on the snout of a wild boar, whose stuffed and mounted head adorned the verandah wall. Being the only boy in the house, I was at first blamed for this prank; but a day or two later, when the spectacles disappeared again only to be discovered dangling from the wires of the parrot's cage, it was agreed that some other agency was at work.

Grandfather was the next to be troubled. He went into the garden one morning to find all his prized sweet peas snipped off and lying on the ground.

Uncle Ken was the next to suffer. He was a heavy sleeper, and once he'd gone to bed, he hated being woken up. So when he came to the breakfast table looking bleary-eyed and miserable, we asked him if he wasn't feeling all right.

'I couldn't sleep a wink last night,' he complained. 'Every time I was about to fall asleep, the bedclothes would be pulled off the bed. I had to get up at least a dozen times to pick them off the floor.' He stared balefully at me. 'Where were you sleeping last night, young man?'

I had an alibi. 'In Grandfather's room,' I said.

'That's right,' said Grandfather. 'And I'm a light sleeper. I'd have woken up if he'd been sleep-walking.'

'It's that ghost from the peepul tree,' said Grandmother.

'It has moved into the house. First my spectacles, then the sweet peas, and now Ken's bedclothes! What will it be up to next? I wonder!'

We did not have to wonder for long. There followed a series of disasters. Vases fell off tables, pictures came down the walls. Parrot feathers turned up in the teapot while the parrot himself let out indignant squawks in the middle of the night. Uncle Ken found a crow's nest in his bed, and on tossing it out of the window was attacked by two crows.

When Aunt Minnie came to stay, things got worse. The pret seemed to take an immediate dislike to Aunt Minnie. She was a nervous, easily excitable person, just the right sort of prey for a spiteful ghost. Somehow her toothpaste got switched with a tube of Grandfather's shaving-cream, and when she appeared in the sitting-room, foaming at the mouth, we ran for our lives. Uncle Ken was shouting that she'd got rabies.

Two days later Aunt Minnie complained that she had been

hit on the nose by a grapefruit, which had of its own accord taken a leap from the pantry shelf and hurtled across the room straight at her. A bruised and swollen nose testified to the attack. Aunt Minnie swore that life had been more peaceful in Upper Burma.

'We'll have to leave this house,' declared Grandmother.

'If we stay here much longer, both Ken and Minnie will have nervous breakdowns.'

'I thought Aunt Minnie broke down long ago,' I said.

'None of your cheek!' snapped Aunt Minnie.

'Anyway, I agree about changing the house,' I said breezily. 'I can't even do my homework. The ink-bottle is always empty.'

'There was ink in the soup last night.' That came from Grandfather.

And so, a few days and several disasters later, we began moving to a new house.

Two bullock-carts laden with furniture and heavy luggage were sent ahead. The roof of the old car was piled high with bags and kitchen utensils. Everyone squeezed into the car, and Grandfather took the driver's seat.

We were barely out of the gate when we heard a peculiar sound, as if someone was chuckling and talking to himself on the roof of the car.

'Is the parrot out there on the luggage-rack?' the query came from Grandfather.

'No, he's in the cage on one of the bullock-carts,' said Grandmother.

Grandfather stopped the car, got out, and took a look at the roof.

'Nothing up there,' he said, getting in again and starting the engine. 'I'm sure I heard the parrot talking.'

Grandfather had driven some way up the road when the chuckling started again, followed by a squeaky little voice.

We all heard it. It was the pret talking to itself.

'Let's go, let's go!' it squeaked gleefully. 'A new house. I can't wait to see it. What fun we're going to have!'

A TRAVELLER'S TALE

Gopalpur-on-sea!
A name to conjure with... And as a boy I'd heard it mentioned, by my father and others, and described as a quaint little seaside resort with a small port on the Orissa coast. The years passed, and I went from boyhood to manhood and eventually old age (is seventy-six old age? I wouldn't know) and still it was only a place I'd heard about and dreamt about but never visited.

Until last month, when I was a guest of KiiT International School in Bhubaneswar, and someone asked me where I'd like to go, and I said, 'Is Gopalpur very far?'

And off I went, along a plam-fringed highway, through busy little market-towns with names Rhamba and Humma, past the enormous Chilka lake which opens into the sea through paddy fields and keora plantations, and finally on to Gopalpur's beach road, with the sun glinting like gold on the great waves of the ocean, and the fishermen counting their catch, and the children sprinting into the sea, tumbling about in the shallows.

But the seafront wore a neglected look. The hotels were empty, the cafés deserted. A cheeky crow greeted me with a disconsolate caw from its perch on a weathered old wall. Some of the buildings were recent, but around us there were also the shells of older buildings that had fallen into ruin. And no one was going to preserve these relics of a colonial past. A small house called 'Brighton Villa' still survived.

But away from the seafront a tree-lined road took us past some well-maintained bungalows, a school, an old cemetery, and finally a PWD rest house where we were to spend the night.

It was growing dark when we arrived, and in the twilight I could just make out the shapes of the trees that surround the old bungalow—a hoary old banyan, a jack-fruit and several mango trees. The light from the bungalow's veranda fell on some oleander bushes. A hawk moth landed on my shirt-front and appeared reluctant to leave. I took it between my fingers and deposited it on the oleander bush.

It was almost midnight when I went to bed. The rest-house staff—the caretaker and the gardener—went to some trouble to arrange a meal, but it was a long time coming. The gardener told me the house had once been the residence of an Englishman who had left the country at the time of Independence, some sixty years or more ago. Some changes had been carried out, but the basic structure remained—high-ceilinged rooms with skylights, a long verandah and enormous bathrooms. The bathroom was so large you could have held a party in it. But there was just one potty and a basin. You could sit on the potty and meditate, fixing your thoughts (or absence of thought) on the distant basin.

I closed all doors and windows, switched off all lights (I find it impossible to sleep with a light on), and went to bed.

It was a comfortable bed, and I soon fell asleep. Only to be awakened by a light tapping on the window near my bed.

Probably a branch of the oleander bush, I thought, and fell asleep again. But there was more tapping, louder this time, and then I was fully awake.

I sat up in bed and drew aside the curtains.

There was a face at the window.

In the half-light from the verandah I could not make out the features, but it was definitely a human face.

Obviously someone wanted to come in, the caretaker perhaps, or the chowkidar. But then, why not knock on the door? Perhaps he had. The door was at the other end of the room, and I may not have heard the knocking.

I am not in the habit of opening my doors to strangers in the night, but somehow I did not feel threatened or uneasy, so I got up, unlatched the door, and opened it for my midnight visitor.

Standing on the threshold was an imposing figure.

A tall dark man, turbaned, and dressed all in white. He wore some sort of uniform—the kind worn by those immaculate doormen at five-star hotels; but a rare sight in Gopalpur-on-sea.

'What is it you want?' I asked. 'Are you staying here?'

He did not reply but looked past me, possibly through me, and then walked silently into the room. I stood there, bewildered and awestruck, as he strode across to my bed, smoothed out the sheets and patted down my pillow. He then walked over to the next room and came back with a glass and a jug of water, which he placed on the bedside table. As if that were not enough, he picked up my day clothes, folded them neatly and placed them on a vacant chair. Then, just as unobtrusively and without so much as a glance in my direction, he left the room and walked out into the night.

Early next morning, as the sun came up like thunder over the Bay of Bengal, I went down to the sea again, picking my way over the puddles of human excreta that decorated parts of the beach. Well, you can't have everything. The world might be more beautiful without the human presence; but then, who would appreciate it?

Back at the rest house for breakfast, I was reminded of my visitor of the previous night.

'Who was the tall gentleman who came to my room last night?' I asked. 'He looked like a butler. Smartly dressed, very dignified.'

The caretaker and the gardener exchanged meaningful glances.

'You tell him,' said the caretaker to his companion.

'It must have been Hazoor Ali,' said the gardener, nodding. 'He was the orderly, the personal servant of Mr Robbins, the port commissioner—the Englishman who lived here.'

'But that was over sixty years ago,' I said. 'They must all be dead.'

'Yes, all are dead, sir. But sometimes the ghost of Hazoor Ali appears, especially if one of our guests reminds him of his old master. He was quite devoted to him, sir. In fact, he received this bungalow as a parting gift when Mr Robbins left the country. But unable to maintain it, he sold it to the government and returned to his home in Cuttack. He died many years ago, but revisits this place sometimes. Do not feel alarmed, sir. He means no harm. And he does not appear to everyone—you are the lucky one this year! I have but seen him twice. Once, when I took service here twenty years ago, and then, last year, the night before the cyclone. He came to warn us, I think. Went to every door and window and made sure they were secured. Never said a word. Just vanished into the night.'

'And it's time for me to vanish by day,' I said, getting my things ready. I had to be in Bhubaneswar by late afternoon, to board the plane for Delhi. I was sorry it had been such a short stay. I would have liked to spend a few days in Gopalpur, wandering about its backwaters, old roads, mango groves, fishing villages, sandy inlets… Another time perhaps. In this life, if I am so lucky. Or the next, if I am luckier still.

At the airport in Bhubaneswar, the security asked me for my photo-identity. 'Driving licence, pan-card, passport? Anything with your picture on it will do, since you have an e-ticket,' he explained.

I do not have a driving licence and have never felt the need to carry my pan-card with me. Luckily, I always carry my passport on my travels. I looked for it in my little travel-bag and then in my suitcase, but couldn't find it. I was feeling awkward fumbling in all my pockets, when another senior officer came to my rescue. 'It's all right. Let him in. I know Mr Ruskin Bond,' he called out, and beckoned me inside. I thanked him and hurried into the check-in area.

All the time in the flight, I was trying to recollect where I might have kept my passport. Possibly tucked away somewhere inside the suitcase, I thought. Now that my baggage was sealed at the airport, I decided to look for it when I reached home.

A day later I was back in my home in the hills, tired after a long road journey from Delhi. I like travelling by road, there is so much to see, but the ever-increasing volume of traffic turns it into an obstacle race most of the time. To add to my woes, my passport was still missing. I looked for it everywhere—my suitcase, travel-bag, in all my pockets.

I gave up the search. Either I had dropped it somewhere, or I had left it at Gopalpur. I decided to ring up and check with the rest house staff the next day.

It was a frosty night, bitingly cold, so I went to bed early, well-covered with razai and blanket. Only two nights previously I had been sleeping under a fan!

It was a windy night, the windows were rattling; and the old tin roof was groaning, a loose sheet flapping about and making a frightful din.

I slept only fitfully.

When the wind abated, I heard someone knocking on my front door.

'Who's there?' I called, but there was no answer.

The knocking continued, insistent, growing louder all the time.

'Who's there? *Kaun hai*?' I called again.

Only that knocking.

Someone in distress, I thought. I'd better see who it is. I got up shivering, and walked barefoot to the front door. Opened it slowly, opened it wider, someone stepped out of the shadows.

Hazoor Ali salaamed, entered the room, and as in Gopalpur, he walked silently into the room. It was lying in disarray because of my frantic search for my passport. He arranged the room, removed my garments from my travel-bag, folded them and placed them neatly upon the cupboard shelves. Then, he did a salaam again and waited at the door.

Strange, I thought. If he did the entire room why did he not set the travel-bag in its right place? Why did he leave it lying on the floor? Possibly he didn't know where to keep it; he left the last bit of work for me. I picked up the bag to place it on the top shelf. And there, from its front pocket my passport fell out, on to the floor.

I turned to look at Hazoor Ali, but he had already walked out into the cold darkness.

THE CHAKRATA CAT

The Chakrata is a small hill station roughly midway between Shimla and Mussoorie. During my youth, before the road became motorable, I would trek from one hill station to the other, sometimes alone, sometimes in company. It would take me about five days to cover the distance. I was a leisurely walker. You couldn't enjoy a hike if you felt you had to catch a train at the end of it.

At Chakrata, there was an old forest rest house where I would sometimes spend the night. Don't go looking for it now. It has fallen into disuse and been replaced by a new building closer to the town.

Towards sunset, late that summer, I trudged upto the rest house and called out for the chowkidar. I forgot his name. He was a grizelled old man, uncommunicative. If you told him you had just been chased by a bear, he would simply nod and say, 'You'd better rest, then. You must be tired.' Nothing about the bear!

Anyway, he opened up one of the bedrooms for me, prepared a modest meal (which enjoyed, having eaten little all day), and offered to make a fire in the old fireplace.

Chakrata can be cold, even in September, and I offered to

pay for the firewood if he would fetch some. He switched on the bedroom and verandah lights and then walked to the rear of the building to fetch some wood.

That was when I saw the cat.

It was a large black cat, and it was sitting before the fireplace, almost as though expecting a fire to be lit. I hadn't noticed it entering the room, and it did not pay much attention to me, just kept staring into the fireplace. Then, when it heard the chowkidar returning, it got up and left the room.

'You have a cat?' I asked, trying to make conversation while he lit the fire.

He stood his head. 'Cats come for rats,' he said, which left me no wiser. And he took off, promising to bring me a cup of tea early next morning. There was a small bookshelf in a corner of a room, and I found an old favourite, *A Warning to the Curious* by M.R. James. His haunting stories of ghosts in old colleges kept me awake for a couple of hours; then I put out the light and got into bed.

I had quite forgotten about the cat.

Now I heard a soft purring as the cat jumped on to the bed and curled up near my feet. I am not particularly fond of cats, and my first impulse was to kick it off the bed. Then I thought; 'Well, its probably used to sleeping in this room, especially with the fire lit. I'll let it be, as long as it doesn't start chasing rats in the middle in the night!' And all it did was come a little closer to me, advancing from my feet to my knees, and purring loudly, as though quite satisfied with the situation.

I fell asleep and slept soundly. In fact, I must have slept for a couple of hours before I woke to a feeling of wetness under my armpit. My vest was wet, and something was sucking away at my flesh.

It was with a feeling of horror that I realized that the cat had crawled into bed with me, that it was now stretched out beside me, and that it was licking away at my armpit with a certain amount of relish. For the purring was louder than ever.

I sat up in bed, flung the cat from me, and made a dash for the light switch. As the light came on, I saw the cat standing at the foot of the bed, tail erect and hair on end. It was very angry. And then, for the space of five seconds at the most, its appearance changed and its head was that of a human—a woman, black-browed with flaring nostrils and large crooked ears, her lips full and drenched with blood—my blood!

The moment passed and it was a cat's head once again. She let out a howl, sprang from the bed, and disappeared through the bathroom door.

My shirt and vest were soaked with blood. For over an hour the cat had been licking and sucking at my fragile skin, wearing it away until the blood oozed out. Cat or vampire or witches revenant? Or a combination of all three.

I went to the bathroom. The cat had taken off through an open window. I closed the window, bathed my wound, examined myself in the mirror.

I had not been bitten. There were no teeth marks, no scratches. The tongue, and constant licking, had done the damage.

I found some cotton-wool in my haversacks, and used it to stop the trickle of blood from armpit. Then I changed my vest and shirt, and sat down on an easy chair to wait for the dawn. It was three in the morning. I felt weak and fell asleep in my chair, to be wakened by the chowkidar knocking on my door with a cup of tea.

Chakrata is a lovely place, prettier than most hill stations, but

I had no desire to linger there. There was a bus to Dehradun at eight o'clock. I decided to cut short my trek and take the bus.

'Where's that cat of yours?' I asked the chowkidar before I left. He knew nothing about a cat. Did not care for cats. They were unlucky, the companions of evil spirits, creatures of the world of the dead.

I did not stop to argue, but thanked him for his hospitality and took my leave.

The wound, if you can call it that, took some time to heal. The skin beneath my armpit was all crinkly for a few weeks, but the body heals itself, if given a chance to do so.

But what remains on my skin is a bright red mark, the size and shape of a cat's tongue. It's been there all these years and won't go away. I'll show it to you, the next time you come to see me.

A DREADFUL GURGLE

Have you ever woken up in the night to find someone in your bed who wasn't supposed to be there? Well, it happened to me when I was at boarding school in Shimla, many years ago.

I was sleeping in the senior dormitory, along with some twenty other boys, and my bed was positioned in a corner of the long room, at some distance from the others. There was no shortage of pranksters in our dormitory, and one had to look out for the introduction of stinging-nettle or pebbles or possibly even a small lizard under the bedsheets. But I wasn't prepared for a body in my bed.

At first I thought a sleep-walker had mistakenly got into my bed, and I tried to push him out, muttering, 'Devinder, get back into your own bed. There isn't room for two of us.' Devinder was a notorious sleep-walker, who had even ended up on the roof on one occasion.

But it wasn't Devinder.

Devinder was a short boy, and this fellow was a tall, lanky person. His feet stuck out of the blanket at the foot of the bed. *It must be Ranjit*, I thought. Ranjit had huge feet.

'Ranjit,' I hissed. 'Stop playing the fool, and get back to

your own bed.'

No response.

I tried pushing, but without success. The body was heavy and inert. It was also very cold.

I lay there wondering who it could be, and then it began to dawn on me that the person beside me wasn't breathing, and the horrible realization came to me that there was a corpse in my bed. How did it get there, and what was I to do about it?

'Vishal,' I called out to a boy who was sleeping a short distance away. 'Vishal, wake up, there's a corpse in the bed!'

Vishal did wake up. 'You're dreaming, Bond. Go to sleep and stop disturbing everyone.'

Just then there was a groan followed by a dreadful gurgle, from the body beside me. I shot out of the bed, shouting at the top of my voice, waking up the entire dormitory.

Lights came on. There was total confusion. The Housemaster came running. I told him and everyone else what had happened. They came to my bed and had a good look at it. But there was no one there.

On my insistence, I was moved to the other end of the dormitory. The house prefect, Johnson, took over my former bed. Two nights passed without further excitement, and a couple of boys started calling me a funk and a scaredy-cat. My response was to punch one of them on the nose.

Then, on the third night, we were all woken by several ear-splitting shrieks, and Johnson came charging across the dormitory, screaming that two icy hands had taken him by the throat and tried to squeeze the life out of him. Lights came on, and the poor old Housemaster came dashing in again. We calmed Johnson down and put him in a spare bed. The Housemaster shone his torch on the boy's face and neck, and sure enough, we saw several bruises on his flesh and the outline of a large hand.

Next day, the offending bed was removed from the dormitory, but it was a few days before Johnson recovered from the shock. He was kept in the infirmary until the bruises disappeared. But for the rest of the year he was a nervous wreck.

Our nursing sister, who had looked after the infirmary for many years, recalled that some twenty years earlier, a boy called Tomkins had died suddenly in the dormitory. He was very tall for his age, but apparently suffered from a heart problem. That day he had taken part in a football match, and had gone to bed looking pale and exhausted. Early next morning, when the bell rang for morning gym, he was found stiff and cold, having died during the night.

'He died peacefully, poor boy,' recalled our nursing sister.

But I'm not so sure. I can still hear that dreadful gurgle from the body in my bed. And there was the struggle with Johnson. No, there was nothing peaceful about that death. Tomkins had gone most unwillingly…

THE WHITE PIGEON

About fifty years ago in Dehradun, there lived a very happily married couple—an English colonel and his wife. They were both enthusiastic gardeners and their beautiful bungalow was covered with bougainvillea, while in the garden, the fragrance of the jasmine challenged the sweet fragrance of the honeysuckle. They had lived together many years when the wife suddenly became very ill. Nothing could be done for her. As she lay dying, she told her family and her servants that she would return to the garden in the form of a white pigeon, so that she could be near her husband and the place she had loved so dearly.

Years passed, but no white pigeon appeared. The colonel was lonely; and when he met an attractive widow, a few years younger to him, he married her and brought her home to his beautiful house. But as he was carrying his new bride through the porch and up the verandah steps, a white pigeon came fluttering into the garden and perched on a jasmine bush. There it remained for a long time, cooing and murmuring in a sad, subdued manner.

Afterwards, it entered the garden everyday and alighted on the jasmine bush, where it would call sadly and persistently. The servants became upset and frightened. They remembered the dying promise of their former mistress, and they were convinced that her spirit dwelt in the white pigeon.

When she heard the story, the Colonel's new wife was very upset. When the Colonel saw how troubled she was, he decided to do something about it. So when the pigeon appeared the next day, he took his gun and slipped out of the house, stealthily making his way down the verandah steps. When he saw the pigeon on the jasmine bush, he raised his gun and fired.

There was a woman's high-pitched scream. And then the pigeon flew away, its white breast dark with blood.

That same night the Colonel died in his sleep. No one ever knew the reason for his sudden death. When I looked up the cause of death in the local Burial Register, I saw that it had been given as 'respiratory failure'. In other words, he had just stopped breathing!

The Colonel's widow left Dehradun, and the beautiful bungalow fell into ruin. You can still see the ruins on the banks of the Bindal watercourse. The garden has become a jungle, and jackals slink through the roofless rooms.

The Colonel was buried in the grounds of his estate, and the gravestone is still there, although the inscription has long since disappeared.

Few people pass that way. But those who do say that they have often seen a white pigeon resting on the grave, and that on its white breast a crimson stain could be noticed.

HE WHO RIDES A TIGER

To the boatmen of the Hooghly and the woodcutters and honey-gatherers of the Sunderbans, 'Gazi Saheb' is a name that is still invoked in times of storm or stress. Stories of the magical powers of this wonderful fakir have come down to us in song and legend.

In the south of Calcutta where the town of Baruipur now stands, there was once a dense, impenetrable jungle laced with crocodile-infested creeks. Into this wasteland came a fakir, Mobrah Gazi by name, to take up his residence at a place called Basra. He so overawed the wild animals that they became his servants, and the 'Gazi Saheb' (as he came to be known) was often seen riding about on a tiger.

It is said that the zamindar of the pargana in which Basra was situated was placed under arrest because he was unable to pay the annual revenue to the emperor at Delhi. The zamindar's mother, fearing for her son's life, sought the assistance of the great Gazi. The fakir promised his aid.

After sending the woman home, he dismounted from his royal Bengal tiger and sat down in deep meditation. So great were his powers that his thoughts were telegraphed over the many hundred miles separating his jungle from Delhi and he gave the emperor a dream in which he, Gazi Saheb, appeared surrounded by wild beasts, saying that he was the proprietor of the Basra jungles and that the zamindar's dues would be paid from his own treasures buried in the forest. He told the emperor to have the zamindar released, threatening him with every misfortune if he disobeyed.

The emperor awoke late the next morning and, overtaken by the business of his court, forgot the dream. The following morning when he ascended his throne, instead of seeing the usual courtiers and attendants, he found himself surrounded by wild animals. He immediately remembered the dream and in great haste ordered the release of the zamindar. The animals vanished. A few weeks later, the revenue arrived, paid out of the Gazi's treasure.

In gratitude for the Gazi's aid, the zamindar erected a mosque in the jungles of Basra as a residence for the saint but the Gazi Saheb, who had no use for material possessions and used his mysterious treasure only to assist others, said that he preferred the shelter of the forests in the sunshine and rain and desired neither a mosque nor house. The zamindar then ordered that every village in his zamindari should erect an altar dedicated to Gazi Saheb, 'King of the Sunderbans and of the Wild Beasts,' and warned his tenants that if they failed to make an offering before going into the jungle they would almost certainly be devoured by tigers or crocodiles.

And so, even today, between Calcutta and the sea, the Gazi Saheb is recognized as a saint in many of the villages of the Sunderbans and his name is held in reverence by both Hindus and Muslims.

There is no record of the Gazi Saheb ever having taken a wife, yet there are a number of fakirs who call themselves his descendants, gaining a livelihood from the offerings of boatmen and woodcutters. That they do not have the powers of the original Gazi have been proved more than once, for it is usually the fakirs and not the village folk who are carried off by tigers or crocodiles.

Many people have tried to ascertain the whereabouts of the tomb of Gazi Saheb. Some declare it lies near Baruipur where the saint first took up his abode. Others say that it is to be found in the jungles of Sagar Island by the creek that runs into the sea. And there are some who feel sure that there is no tomb and that the Gazi Saheb left this earth in no ordinary way but was taken to paradise, riding on the back of a royal Bengal tiger.

THE WIND ON HAUNTED HILL

Whoo, whoo, whoo, cried the wind as it swept down from the Himalayan snows. It hurried over the hills and passes and hummed and moaned through the tall pines and deodars. There was little on Haunted Hill to stop the wind-only a few stunted trees and bushes and the ruins of a small settlement.

On the slopes of the next hill was a village. People kept large stones on their tin roofs to prevent them from being blown off. There was nearly always a strong wind in these parts. Three children were spreading clothes out to dry on a low stone wall, putting a stone on each piece.

Eleven-year-old Usha, dark-haired and rose-cheeked, struggled with her grandfather's long, loose shirt. Her younger brother, Suresh, was doing his best to hold down a bedsheet, while Usha's friend, Binya, a slightly older girl, helped.

Once everything was firmly held down by stones, they climbed up on the flat rocks and sat there sunbathing and staring across the fields at the ruins on Haunted Hill.

'I must go to the bazaar today,' said Usha.

'I wish I could come too,' said Binya. 'But I have to help with the cows.'

'I can come!' said eight-year-old Suresh. He was always ready to visit the bazaar, which was three miles away, on the other side of the hill.

'No, you can't,' said Usha. 'You must help Grandfather chop wood.'

'Won't you feel scared returning alone?' he asked. 'There are ghosts on Haunted Hill!'

'I'll be back before dark. Ghosts don't appear during the day.'

'Are there lots of ghosts in the ruins?' asked Binya.

'Grandfather says so. He says that over a hundred years ago, some Britishers lived on the hill. But the settlement was always being struck by lightning, so they moved away.'

'But if they left, why is the place visited by ghosts?'

'Because—Grandfather says—during a terrible storm, one of the houses was hit by lightning, and everyone in it was killed. Even the children.'

'How many children?'

'Two. A boy and his sister. Grandfather saw them playing there in the moonlight.'

'Wasn't he frightened?'

'No. Old people don't mind ghosts.'

Usha set out for the bazaar at two in the afternoon. It was about an hour's walk. The path went through yellow fields of flowering mustard, then along the saddle of the hill, and up, straight through the ruins. Usha had often gone that way to shop at the bazaar or to see her aunt, who lived in the town nearby.

Wild flowers bloomed on the crumbling walls of the ruins, and a wild plum tree grew straight out of the floor of what had once been a hall. It was covered with soft, white blossoms. Lizards scuttled over the stones, while a whistling thrush, its deep purple plumage glistening in the sunshine, sat on a window-sill and sang its heart out.

Usha sang too, as she skipped lightly along the path, which clipped steeply down to the valley and led to the little town with its quaint bazaar.

Moving leisurely, Usha bought spices, sugar and matches. With the two rupees she had saved from her pocket-money, she chose a necklace of amber-coloured beads for herself and some marbles for Suresh. Then she had her mother's slippers repaired at a cobbler's shop.

Finally, Usha went to visit Aunt Lakshmi at her flat above the shops. They were talking and drinking cups of hot, sweet tea when Usha realized that dark clouds had gathered over the mountains. She quickly picked up her things, said goodbye to her aunt, and set out for the village.

Strangely, the wind had dropped. The trees were still, the crickets silent. The crows flew round in circles, then settled in an oak tree.

'I must get home before dark,' thought Usha, hurrying along the path.

But the sky had darkened and a deep rumble echoed over the hills. Usha felt the first heavy drop of rain hit her cheek. Holding the shopping bag close to her body, she quickened her pace until she was almost running. The raindrops were coming down faster now—cold, stinging pellets of rain. A flash of lightning sharply outlined the ruins on the hill, and then all was dark again. Night had fallen.

'I'll have to shelter in the ruins,' Usha thought and began to run. Suddenly the wind sprang up again, but she did not have to fight it. It was behind her now, helping her along, up the steep path and on to the brow of the hill. There was another flash of lightning, followed by a peal of thunder. The ruins loomed before her, grim and forbidding.

Usha remembered part of an old roof that would give some shelter. It would be better than trying to go on. In the dark, with the howling wind, she might stray off the path and fall over the edge of the cliff.

'Whoo, whoo, whoo…' howled the wind. Usha saw the wild plum tree swaying, its foliage thrashing against the ground. She found her way into the ruins, helped by the constant flicker of lightning. Usha placed her hands flat against a stone wall and moved sideways, hoping to reach the sheltered corner. Suddenly, her hand touched something soft and furry, and she gave a startled cry. Her cry was answered by another—half snarl, half screech—as something leapt away in the darkness.

With a sigh of relief Usha realized that it was the cat that lived in the ruins. For a moment she had been frightened, but now she moved quickly along the wall until she heard the rain drumming on a remnant of a tin roof. Crouched in a corner, she found some shelter. But the tin sheet groaned and clattered as if it would sail away any moment.

Usha remembered that across this empty room stood an old fireplace. Perhaps it would be drier there under the blocked chimney. But she would not attempt to find it just now—she might lose her way altogether.

Her clothes were soaked and water streamed down from her hair, forming a puddle at her feet. She thought she heard a faint cry—the cat again, or an owl? Then the storm blotted out all other sounds.

There had been no time to think of ghosts, but now that she was settled in one place, Usha remembered Grandfather's story about the lightning blasted ruins. She hoped and prayed that lightning would not strike her.

Thunder boomed over the hills, and the lightning came

quicker now. Then there was a bigger flash, and for a moment the entire ruin was lit up. A streak of blue sizzled along the floor of the building. Usha was staring straight ahead, and, as the opposite wall lit up, she saw, crouching in front of the unused fireplace, two small figures—children!

The ghostly figures seemed to look up and stare back at Usha. And then everything was dark again.

Usha's heart was in her mouth. She had seen without doubt, two ghosts on the other side of the room. She wasn't going to remain in the ruins one minute longer.

She ran towards the big gap in the wall through which she had entered. She was halfway across the open space when something—someone—fell against her. Usha stumbled, got up, and again bumped into something. She gave a frightened scream. Someone else screamed. And then there was a shout, a boy's shout, and Usha instantly recognized the voice.

'Suresh!'

'Usha!'

'Binya!'

They fell into each other's arms, so surprised and relieved that all they could do was laugh and giggle and repeat each other's names.

Then Usha said, 'I thought you were ghosts.'

'We thought you were a ghost,' said Suresh.

'Come back under the roof,' said Usha.

They huddled together in the corner, chattering with excitement and relief.

'When it grew dark, we came looking for you,' said Binya. 'And then the storm broke.'

'Shall we run back together?' asked Usha. 'I don't want to stay here any longer.'

'We'll have to wait,' said Binya. 'The path has fallen away at one place. It won't be safe in the dark, in all this rain.'

'We'll have to wait till morning,' said Suresh, 'and I'm so hungry!'

The storm continued, but they were not afraid now. They gave each other warmth and confidence. Even the ruins did not seem so forbidding.

After an hour the rain stopped, and the thunder grew more distant.

Towards dawn the whistling thrush began to sing. Its sweet, broken notes flooded the ruins with music. As the sky grew lighter, they saw that the plum tree stood upright again, though it had lost all its blossoms.

'Let's go,' said Usha.

Outside the ruins, walking along the brow of the hill, they watched the sky grow pink. When they were some distance away, Usha looked back and said, 'Can you see something behind the wall? It's like a hand waving.'

'It's just the top of the plum tree,' said Binya.

'Goodbye, goodbye...' They heard voices.

'Who said "goodbye"?' asked Usha.

'Not I,' said Suresh.

'Not I,' said Binya.

'I heard someone calling,' said Usha.

'It's only the wind,' assured Binya.

Usha looked back at the ruins. The sun had come up and was touching the top of the wall.

'Come on,' said Suresh. 'I'm hungry.'

They hurried along the path to the village.

'Goodbye, goodbye...' Usha heard them calling. Was it just the wind?

A JOB WELL DONE

Dhuki, the gardener, was clearing up the weeds that grew in profusion around the old disused well. He was an old man, skinny and bent and spindly-legged; but he had always been like that; his strength lay in his wrists and in his long, tendril-like fingers. He looked as frail as a petunia, but he had the tenacity of a vine.

'Are you going to cover the well?' I asked. I was eight, a great favourite of Dhuki. He had been the gardener long before my birth; had worked for my father, until my father died, and now worked for my mother and stepfather.

'I must cover it, I suppose,' said Dhuki. 'That's what the 'Major Sahib' wants. He'll be back any day, and if he finds the well still uncovered, he'll get into one of his raging fits and I'll be looking for another job!'

The 'Major Sahib' was my stepfather, Major Summerskill. A tall, hearty, back-slapping man, who liked polo and pig-sticking. He was quite unlike my father. My father had always given me books to read. The Major said I would become a dreamer if I read too much, and took the books away. I hated him and did not think much of my mother for marrying him.

'The boy's too soft,' I heard him tell my mother. 'I must

see that he gets riding lessons.'

But before the riding lessons could be arranged, the Major's regiment was ordered to Peshawar. Trouble was expected from some of the frontier tribes. He was away for about two months. Before leaving, he had left strict instructions for Dhuki to cover up the old well.

'Too damned dangerous having an open well in the middle of the garden,' my stepfather had said. 'Make sure that it's completely covered by the time I get back.'

Dhuki was loath to cover up the old well. It had been there for over fifty years, long before the house had been built. In its walls lived a colony of pigeons. Their soft cooing filled the garden with a lovely sound. And during the hot, dry, summer months, when taps ran dry, the well was always a dependable source of water. The bhisti still used it, filling his goatskin bag with the cool clear water and sprinkling the paths around the house to keep the dust down.

Dhuki pleaded with my mother to let him leave the well uncovered.

'What will happen to the pigeons?' he asked.

'Oh, surely they can find another well,' said my mother. 'Do close it up soon, Dhuki. I don't want the Sahib to come back and find that you haven't done anything about it.'

My mother seemed just a little bit afraid of the Major. How can we be afraid of those we love? It was a question that puzzled me then, and puzzles me still.

The Major's absence made life pleasant again. I returned to my books, spent long hours in my favourite banyan tree, ate buckets of mangoes, and dawdled in the garden talking to Dhuki.

Neither he nor I were looking forward to the Major's return. Dhuki had stayed on after my mother's second marriage only out of loyalty to her and affection for me; he had really been my father's man. But my mother had always appeared deceptively frail and helpless, and most men, Major Summerskill included, felt protective towards her. She liked people who did things for her.

'Your father liked this well,' said Dhuki. 'He would often sit here in the evenings, with a book in which he made drawings of birds and flowers and insects.'

I remembered those drawings, and I remembered how they had all been thrown away by the Major when he had moved into the house. Dhuki knew about it, too. I didn't keep much from him.

'It's a sad business closing this well,' said Dhuki again. 'Only a fool or a drunkard is likely to fall into it.'

But he had made his preparations. Planks of sal wood, bricks and cement were neatly piled up around the well.

'Tomorrow,' said Dhuki. 'Tomorrow I will do it. Not today. Let the birds remain for one more day. In the morning, Baba, you can help me drive the birds from the well.

On the day my stepfather was expected back, my mother hired a tonga and went to the bazaar to do some shopping. Only a few people had cars in those days. Even colonels went about in tongas. Now, a clerk finds it beneath his dignity to sit in one.

As the Major was not expected before evening, I decided I would make full use of my last free morning. I took all my favourite books and stored them away in an outhouse where I could come for them from time to time. Then, my pockets bursting with mangoes, I climbed into the banyan tree. It was the darkest and coolest place on a hot day in June.

From behind the screen of leaves that concealed me, I could see Dhuki moving about near the well. He appeared to be most unwilling to get on with the job of covering it up.

'Baba!' he called, several times; but I did not feel like stirring from the banyan tree. Dhuki grasped a long plank of wood and placed it across one end of the well. He started hammering. From my vantage point in the banyan tree, he looked very bent and old.

A jingle of tonga bells and the squeak of unoiled wheels told me that a tonga was coming in at the gate. It was too early for my mother to be back. I peered through the thick, waxy leaves of the tree, and nearly fell off my branch in surprise. It was my stepfather, the Major! He had arrived earlier than expected.

I did not come down from the tree. I had no intention of confronting my stepfather until my mother returned.

The Major had climbed down from the tonga and was watching his luggage being carried on to the verandah. He was red in the face and the ends of his handlebar moustache were stiff with brilliantine. Dhuki approached with a half-hearted salaam.

'Ah, so there you are, you old scoundrel!' exclaimed the Major, trying to sound friendly and jocular. 'More jungle than garden, from what I can see. You're getting too old for this sort of work, Dhuki. Time to retire! And where's the Memsahib?'

'Gone to the bazaar,' said Dhuki.

'And the boy?'

Dhuki shrugged. 'I have not seen the boy, today, Sahib.'

'Damn!' said the Major. 'A fine homecoming, this is. Well, wake up the cook-boy and tell him to get some sodas.'

'Cook-boy's gone away,' said Dhuki.

'Well, I'll be double-damned,' said the major.

The tonga went away, and the Major started pacing up and down the garden path. Then he saw Dhuki's unfinished work at the well. He grew purple in the face, strode across to the well, and started ranting at the old gardener.

Dhuki began making excuses. He said something about a shortage of bricks; the sickness of a niece; unsatisfactory cement; unfavourable weather; unfavourable gods. When none of this seemed to satisfy the Major, Dhuki began mumbling about something bubbling up from the bottom of the well, and pointed down into its depths. The Major stepped on to the low parapet and looked down. Dhuki kept pointing. The Major leant over a little.

Dhuki's hands moved swiftly, like a conjurer's making a pass. He did not actually push the Major. He appeared merely to tap him once on the bottom. I caught a glimpse of my stepfather's boots as he disappeared into the well. I couldn't help thinking of *Alice's Adventures in Wonderland*, of Alice disappearing down the rabbit hole.

There was a tremendous splash, and the pigeons flew up, circling the well thrice before settling on the roof of the bungalow.

By lunch time—or tiffin, as we called it then—Dhuki had the well covered over with the wooden planks.

'The Major will be pleased,' said my mother, when she came home. 'It will be quite ready by evening, won't it, Dhuki?'

By evening, the well had been completely bricked over. It was the fastest bit of work Dhuki had ever done.

Over the next few weeks, my mother's concern changed to anxiety, her anxiety to melancholy, and her melancholy to resignation. By being gay and high-spirited myself, I hope I did something to cheer her up. She had written to the Colonel of the Regiment, and had been informed that the Major had gone home on leave a fortnight previously. Somewhere, in the vastness of India, the Major had disappeared.

It was easy enough to disappear and never be found. After several months had passed without the Major turning up, it was presumed that one of the two things must have happened. Either he had been murdered on the train, and his corpse flung into a river; or, he had run away with a tribal girl and was living in some remote corner of the country.

Life had to carry on for the rest of us. The rains were over, and the guava season was approaching.

My mother was receiving visits from a colonel of His Majesty's 32nd Foot. He was an elderly, easy-going, seemingly absent-minded man, who didn't get in the way at all, but left slabs of chocolate lying around the house.

'A *good* Sahib,' observed Dhuki, as I stood beside him behind the bougainvillaea, watching the Colonel saunter up the verandah steps. 'See how well he wears his sola-topi! It covers his head completely.'

'He's bald underneath,' I said.

'No matter. I think he will be all right.'

'And if he isn't,' I said, 'we can always open up the well again.'

Dhuki dropped the nozzle of the hosepipe, and water gushed out over our feet. But he recovered quickly, and taking me by the hand, led me across to the old well, now surmounted by a three-tiered cement platform which looked rather like a wedding cake.

'We must not forget our old well,' he said. 'Let us make it beautiful, Baba. Some flower pots, perhaps.'

And together we fetched pots, and decorated the covered well with ferns and geraniums. Everyone congratulated Dhuki on the fine job he'd done. My only regret was that the pigeons had gone away.

A FACE UNDER THE PILLOW

'Camping in the jungle was full of danger,' I remarked. 'You must have felt much safer working in the house.'

'Well, cooking was certainly easier,' said Mehmood. 'But I don't know if it was much safer. The animals couldn't get in, true, but there were ghosts and evil spirits lurking in some of the rooms. I changed my room thrice, but there was always someone—*something*—after me. I don't know if I should tell you this, Baba. You have your own small room and you may start imagining things…'

'I'm not afraid of ghosts, Mehmood.'

'That's because you haven't seen one. Although I'm not sure it was a ghost. And I did not actually see anything. But I felt it all right!'

'You can't *feel* a ghost, Mehmood. At least not in stories.'

'This wasn't a story. It was my first night in Carpet-sahib's house in the jungle. It has a big house with many rooms, and I was given a room of my own. But there was no electricity in that out-of-the way place. We used kerosene lamps or candles.

'I had brought my own razai and blanket, but the mattress was a strange one, and so was the pillow. Not a pillow, really, but an old cushion, very hard and lumpy. It was my first night in that bed, and I was very uncomfortable. The candle burnt itself out, and I was still wide awake. I could see very little, there was just a small window allowing a little moonlight into the room. I was almost asleep when I heard someone groaning beside me. Groaning loudly, as though in pain. But there was no one else in the bed, and no one beneath it.

'The groaning stopped for a time, and then, just as I was about to fall asleep, it started again. Groan, groan, groan. Now it seemed to come from beneath my pillow.

'I turned on my side, and slowly, carefully, I slipped my hand beneath the pillow.

'It encountered a hairy face, a gaping mouth, hollow sockets instead of eyes. Horrible to touch! Not the face of a human, Baba—the face of a *rakshas*!

'I tried to pull my hand away, but it was seized by that terrible mouth. A mouth with long sharp teeth—teeth like daggers! It would have bitten my fingers off if I hadn't screamed and shouted for help.

'Carpet-sahib and his sister and the other servants came running. As they rushed into the room with torches and a lamp, these awful teeth released my hand.

'"Under the pillow!" I screamed. "Under the pillow!"

'They looked under the pillow! But there was nothing there. I showed them my fingers—they were bleeding badly.'

'"A rat must have bitten you," said Carpet-sahib's sister. But she knew it wasn't a rat. And she gave me another room to sleep in.

'And were you all right in the second room?'

'For a couple of nights, Baba. And then it happened again.'

'You put your hand under the pillow again? And the face was there?'

'Not the whole face, Baba. Just something soft and squishy. I thought it was a snail under my pillow. So I got up, lit my lamp, and looked under the pillow.'

'What was it, Mehmood? Tell me quickly.'

'It was an eyeball, Baba. An eye that had been removed from its socket. It was staring up at me. Just an eyeball, staring! I picked it up and threw it out of the window. I threw the pillow away too. Something terrible had happened upon that pillow, I'm sure of it.'

'So it wasn't the room?'

'It wasn't the room. It was the pillow, Baba. Next day I went into town and bought a new pillow, and from then on I slept beautifully every night. Never use a strange cushion or pillow, Baba. Terrible things have happened on pillows. So remember—when you return to school next month, take a new pillow, and don't use anyone else's!'

After listening to Mehmood's story, I was always careful to use my own pillow. Even now, many many years later, I carry my own pillow wherever I go. No hotel pillows for me. You never knew what might be lurking beneath them.

A DEMON FOR WORK

In a village in South India there lived a very rich landlord who owned several villages and many fields; but he was such a great miser that he found it difficult to find tenants who would willingly work on his land, and those who did, gave him a lot of trouble. As a result, he left all his fields unfilled, and even his tanks and water channels dried up. This made him poorer day by day. But he made no effort to obtain the goodwill of his tenants.

One day, a holy man paid him a visit. The landlord poured out his tale of woe.

'These miserable tenants won't do a thing for me,' he complained. 'All my lands are going to waste.'

'My dear good landlord,' said the holy man. 'I think I can help you, if you will repeat a mantra—a few magic words—which I will teach you. If you repeat it for three months, day and night, a wonderful demon will appear before you on the first day of the fourth month. He will willingly be your servant and take upon himself all the work that has been left undone by your wretched tenants. The demon will obey all your orders. You will find him equal to a hundred servants!'

The miserly landlord immediately fell at the feet of the holy man and begged for instruction. The sage gave him the magic words and then went his way. The landlord, greatly pleased, repeated the mantra day and night, for three months, till, on the first day of the fourth month, a magnificent young demon stood before him.

'What can I do for you, master?' he said. 'I am at your command.'

The landlord was taken aback by the sight of the huge monster who stood before him, and by the sound of his terrible voice, but he summoned up enough courage to say, 'You can work for me provided—er—you don't expect any salary.'

'Very well,' said the demon, 'but I have one condition. You must give me enough work to keep me busy all the time. If I have nothing to do, I shall kill you and eat you. Juicy landlords are my favourite dish.'

The landlord, certain that there was enough work to keep several demons busy forever, agreed to these terms. He took the demon to a large tank which had been dry for years, and said: 'You must deepen this tank until it is as deep as the height of two palm trees.'

'As you say, master,' said the demon, and set to work.

The landlord went home, feeling sure that the job would take several weeks. His wife gave him a good dinner, and he was just sitting down in his courtyard to enjoy the evening breeze when the demon arrived, casually remarking that the tank was ready.

'The tank ready!' exclaimed the astonished landlord. 'Why, I thought it would take you several weeks! How shall I keep him busy?' he asked, turning to his wife for aid. 'If he goes on at this rate, he'll soon have an excuse for killing and eating me!'

'You must not lose heart, my husband,' said the landlord's

wife. 'Get all the work you can out of the demon. You'll never find such a good worker again. And when you have no more work for him, let me know—I'll find something to keep him busy.'

The landlord went out to inspect the tank and found that it had been completed to perfection. Then he set the demon to plough all his farm lands, which extended over a number of villages. This was done in two days. He next asked the demon to dig up all the waste land. This was done in less than a day.

'I'm getting hungry,' said the demon. 'Come on, master, give me more work, quickly!'

The landlord felt helpless. 'My dear friend,' he said, 'my wife says she has a little job for you. Do go and see what it is she wants done. When you have finished, you can come and eat me, because I just can't see how I can keep you busy much longer!'

The landlord's wife, who had been listening to them, now came out of the house, holding in her hands a long hair which she had just pulled out of her head.

'Well, my good demon,' she said. 'I have a very light job for you. I'm sure you will do it in a twinkling. Take this hair, and when you have made it perfectly straight, bring it back to me.'

The demon laughed uproariously, but took the hair and went away with it.

All night he sat in a peepul tree, trying to straighten the hair. He kept rolling it against his thighs and then lifting it up to see if it had become straight. But no, it would still bend! By morning the demon was feeling very tired.

Then he remembered that goldsmiths, when straightening metal wires, would heat them over a fire. So he made a fire and placed the hair over it, and in the twinkling of an eye it frizzled and burnt up.

The demon was horrified. He dared not return to the landlord's wife. Not only had he failed to straighten the hair, but he had lost it too. Feeling that he had disgraced himself, he ran away to another part of the land.

So the landlord was rid of his demon. But he had learnt a lesson. He decided that it was better to have tenants working for him than demons, even if it meant paying for their services.

THE OVERCOAT

It was clear frosty weather, and as the moon came up over the Himalayan peaks, I could see that patches of snow still lay on the roads of the hill station. I would have been quite happy in bed, with a book and a hot-water bottle at my side, but I'd promised the Kapadias that I'd go to their party, and I felt it would be churlish of me to stay away. I put on two sweaters, an old football scarf, and an overcoat, and set off down the moonlit road.

It was a walk of just over a mile to the Kapadias' house, and I had covered about half the distance when I saw a girl standing in the middle of the road.

She must have been sixteen or seventeen. She looked rather old-fashioned—long hair, hanging to her waist, and a flummoxy sequined dress, pink and lavender, that reminded me of the photos in my Grandmother's family album. When I went closer, I noticed that she had lovely eyes and a winning smile.

'Good evening,' I said. 'It's a cold night to be out.'

'Are you going to the party?' she asked.

'That's right. And I can see from your lovely dress that you're going, too. Come along, we're nearly there.'

She fell into step beside me and we soon saw lights from

the Kapadias' house shining brightly through the deodars. The girl told me her name was Julie. I hadn't seen her before but, then, I'd only been in the hill station a few months.

There was quite a crowd at the party, and no one seemed to know Julie. Everyone thought she was a friend of mine. I did not deny it. Obviously she was someone who was feeling lonely and wanted to be friendly with people. And she was certainly enjoying herself. I did not see her do much eating or drinking, but she flitted about from one group to another, talking, listening, laughing; and when the music began, she was dancing almost continuously, alone or with partners, it didn't matter which, she was completely wrapped up in the music.

It was almost midnight when I got up to go. I had drunk a fair amount of punch, and I was ready for bed. As I was saying goodnight to my hosts and wishing everyone a merry Christmas, Julie slipped her arm into mine and said she'd be going home, too.

When we were outside I said, 'Where do you live, Julie?'

'At Wolfsburn,' she said. 'At the top of the hill.'

'There's a cold wind,' I said. 'And although your dress is beautiful, it doesn't look very warm. Here, you'd better wear my overcoat. I've plenty of protection.'

She did not protest, and allowed me to slip my overcoat over her shoulders. Then we started out on the walk home. But I did not have to escort her all the way. At about the spot where we had met, she said, 'There's a shortcut from here. I'll just scramble up the hillside.'

'Do you know it well?' I asked. 'It's a very narrow path.'

'Oh, I know every stone on the path. I use it all the time. And besides, it's a really bright night.'

'Well, keep the coat on,' I said. 'I can collect it tomorrow.'

She hesitated for a moment, then smiled and nodded at me. She then disappeared up the hill, and I went home alone.

The next day I walked up to Wolfsburn. I crossed a little brook, from which the house had probably got its name, and entered an open iron gate. But of the house itself little remained. Just a roofless ruin, a pile of stones, a shattered chimney, a few Doric pillars where a verandah had once stood.

Had Julie played a joke on me? Or had I found the wrong house?

I walked around the hill to the mission house where the Taylors lived, and asked old Mrs Taylor if she knew a girl called Julie.

'No, I don't think so,' she said. 'Where does she live?'

'At Wolfsburn, I was told. But the house is just a ruin.'

'Nobody has lived at Wolfsburn for over forty years. The Mackinnons lived there. One of the old families who settled here. But when their girl died...' She stopped and gave me a queer look. 'I think her name was Julie... Anyway, when she died, they sold the house and went away. No one ever lived in it again, and it fell into decay. But it couldn't be the same Julie you're looking for. She died of consumption—there wasn't much you could do about it in those days. Her grave is in the cemetery, just down the road.'

I thanked Mrs Taylor and walked slowly down the road to the cemetery: not really wanting to know any more, but propelled forward almost against my will.

It was a small cemetery under the deodars. You could see the eternal snows of the Himalayas standing out against the pristine blue of the sky. Here lay the bones of forgotten Empire-builders—soldiers, merchants, adventurers, their wives and children. It did not take me long to find Julie's grave. It had a simple headstone with her name clearly outlined on it:

> Julie Mackinnon
> 1923–39
> 'With us one moment,
> Taken the next
> Gone to her Maker,
> Gone to her rest.

Although many monsoons had swept across the cemetery wearing down the stones, they had not touched this little tombstone.

I was turning to leave when I caught a glimpse of something familiar behind the headstone. I walked round to where it lay.

Neatly folded on the grass was my overcoat.

EYES OF THE CAT

I wrote this little story for the schoolgirl who said my stories weren't scary enough. Her comment was 'Not bad', and she gave me seven out of ten.

Her eyes seemed flecked with gold when the sun was on them. And as the sun set over the mountains, drawing a deep red wound across the sky, there was more than gold in Kiran's eyes. There was anger; for she had been cut to the quick by some remarks her teacher had made—the culmination of weeks of insults and taunts.

Kiran was poorer than most of the girls in her class and could not afford the tuitions that had become almost obligatory if one was to pass and be promoted. 'You'll have to spend another year in the ninth,' said Madam. 'And if you don't like that, you can find another school—a school where it won't matter if your blouse is torn and your tunic is old and your shoes are falling apart.' Madam had shown her large teeth in what was supposed to be a good-natured smile, and all the girls had tittered dutifully. Sycophancy had become part of the curriculum in Madam's private academy for girls.

On the way home in the gathering gloom, Kiran's two

companions commiserated with her.

'She's a mean old thing,' said Aarti. 'She doesn't care for anyone but herself.'

'Her laugh reminds me of a donkey braying,' said Sunita, who was more forthright.

But Kiran wasn't really listening. Her eyes were fixed on some point in the far distance, where the pines stood in silhouette against a night sky that was growing brighter every moment. The moon was rising, a full moon, a moon that meant something very special to Kiran, that made her blood tingle and her skin prickle and her hair glow and send out sparks. Her steps seemed to grow lighter, her limbs more sinewy as she moved gracefully, softly over the mountain path.

Abruptly she left her companions at a fork in the road.

'I'm taking the shortcut through the forest,' she said.

Her friends were used to her sudden whims. They knew she was not afraid of being alone in the dark. But Kiran's moods made them feel a little nervous, and now, holding hands, they hurried home along the open road.

The shortcut took Kiran through the dark oak forest. The crooked, tormented branches of the oaks threw twisted shadows across the path. A jackal howled at the moon; a nightjar called from urgency, and her breath came in short, sharp gasps. Bright moonlight bathed the hillside when she reached her home on the outskirts of the village.

Refusing her dinner, she went straight to her small room and flung the window open. Moonbeams crept over the window-sill and over her arms which were already covered with golden hair. Her strong nails had shredded the rotten wood of the window-sill.

Tail swishing and ears pricked, the tawny leopard came

swiftly out of the window, crossed the open field behind the house, and melted into the shadows.

A little later it padded silently through the forest.

Although the moon shone brightly on the tin-roofed town, the leopard knew where the shadows were deepest and merged beautifully with them. An occasional intake of breath, which resulted in a short rasping cough, was the only sound it made.

Madam was returning from dinner at a ladies' club, called the Kitten Club as a sort of foil to the husbands' club affiliations. There were still a few people in the street, and while no one could help noticing Madam, who had the contours of a steam-roller, none saw or heard the predator who had slipped down a side alley and reached the steps of the teacher's house. It sat there silently, waiting with all the patience of an obedient schoolgirl.

When Madam saw the leopard on her steps, she dropped her handbag and opened her mouth to scream; but her voice would not materialize. Nor would her tongue ever be used again, either to savour chicken biryani or to pour scorn upon her pupils, for the leopard had sprung at her throat, broken her neck, and dragged her into the bushes.

In the morning, when Aarti and Sunita set out for school, they stopped as usual at Kiran's cottage and called out to her.

Kiran was sitting in the sun, combing her long black hair.

'Aren't you coming to school today, Kiran?' asked the girls.

'No, I won't bother to go today,' said Kiran. She felt lazy, but pleased with herself, like a contented cat.

'Madam won't be pleased,' said Aarti. 'Shall we tell her you're sick?'

'It won't be necessary,' said Kiran, and gave them one of her mysterious smiles. 'I'm sure it's going to be a holiday.'

THE PERFECT MURDER

Stacy Aumonier

One evening in November two brothers were seated in a little café in the Rue de la Roquette discussing murders. The evening papers lay in front of them, and they all contained a lurid account of a shocking affair in the Landes district, where a charcoal-burner had killed his wife and two children with a hatchet. From discussing this murder in particular they went on to discussing murder in general.

'I've never yet read a murder case without being impressed by the extraordinary clumsiness of it,' remarked Paul, the younger brother. 'Here's this fellow who murders his victims with his own hatchet, leaves his hat behind in the shed, and arrives at a village hard by with blood on his boots.'

'They lose their heads,' said Henri, the elder. 'In cases like that they are mentally unbalanced, hardly responsible for their actions.'

'Yes,' replied Paul, 'but what impresses me is—what a lot of murders must be done by people who take trouble, who leave not a trace behind.'

Henri shrugged his shoulders. 'I shouldn't think it was so easy, old boy; there's always something that crops up.'

'Nonsense! I'll guarantee there are thousands done every year. If you are living with anyone, for instance, it must be the easiest thing in the world to murder them.'

'How?'

'Oh, some kind of accident—and then you go screaming into the street, "Oh, my poor wife! Help!" You burst into tears, and everyone consoles you. I read of a woman somewhere who murdered her husband by leaving the window near the bed open at night when he was suffering from pneumonia. Who's going to suspect a case like that? Instead of that, people must always select revolvers, or knives, or go and buy poison at the chemist's across the way.'

'It sounds as though you were contemplating a murder yourself,' laughed Henri.

'Well, you never know,' answered Paul; 'circumstances might arise when a murder would be the only way out of a difficulty. If ever my time comes I shall take a lot of trouble about it. I promise you I shall leave no trace behind.'

As Henri glanced at his brother making this remark he was struck by the fact that there was indeed nothing irreconcilable between the idea of a murder and the idea of Paul doing it. He was a big, saturnine-looking gentleman with a sallow, dissolute face, framed in a black square beard and swathes of untidy grey hair. His profession was that of a traveller in cheap jewellery, and his business dealings were not always of the straightest. Henri shuddered. With his own puny physique, bad health, and vacillating will, he was always dominated by his younger brother. He himself was a clerk in a drapery store, and he had a wife and three children. Paul was unmarried.

The brothers saw a good deal of each other, and were very intimate. But the word friendship would be an extravagant term to apply to their relationship. They were both always hard up, and they borrowed money from each other when every other source failed.

They had no other relatives except a very old uncle and aunt who lived at Chantilly. This uncle and aunt, whose name was Taillandier, were fairly well off, but they would have little to do with the two nephews. They were occasionally invited there to dinner, but neither Paul nor Henri ever succeeded in extracting a franc out of Uncle Robert. He was a very religious man, hard-fisted, cantankerous, and intolerant. His wife was a little more pliable. She was in effect an eccentric. She had spasms of generosity, during which periods both the brothers had at times managed to get money out of her. But these were rare occasions. Moreover, the old man kept her so short of cash that she found it difficult to help her nephews even if she desired to.

As stated, the discussion between the two brothers occurred in November. It was presumably forgotten by both of them immediately afterwards. And indeed, there is no reason to believe that it would ever have recurred, except for certain events which followed the sudden death of Uncle Robert in the February of the following year.

In the meantime, the affairs of both Paul and Henri had gone disastrously. Paul had been detected in a dishonest transaction over a paste trinket, and had just been released from a period of imprisonment. The knowledge of this had not reached his uncle before his death. Henri's wife had had another baby, and had been very ill. He was more in debt than ever.

The news of the uncle's death came as a gleam of hope in the darkness of despair. What kind of will had he left? Knowing their uncle, each was convinced that, however it was framed there was likely to be little or nothing for them. However, the old villain might have left them a thousand or two. And in any case, if the money was all left to the wife, here was a possible field of plunder. It need hardly be said that they repaired with all haste to the funeral, and even with greater alacrity to the lawyer's reading of the will.

The will contained surprises both encouraging and discouraging. In the first place the old man left a considerably larger fortune than anyone could have anticipated. In the second place all the money and securities were carefully tied up, and placed under the control of trustees. There were large bequests to religious charities, whilst the residue was held in trust for his wife. But so far as the brothers were concerned the surprise came at the end. On her death this residue was still to be held in trust, but a portion of the interest was to be divided between Henri and Paul, and on their death to go to the Church. The old man had recognized a certain call of the blood after all!

They both behaved with tact and discretion at the funeral, and were extremely sympathetic and solicitous towards Aunt Rosalie, who was too absorbed with her own trouble to take much notice of them. It was only when it came to the reading of the will that their avidity and interest outraged perhaps the strict canons of good taste. It was Paul who managed to get it clear from the notary what the exact amount would probably be. Making allowances for fluctuations, accidents, and acts of God, on the death of Mme Taillandier the two brothers would inherit something between eight and ten thousand francs a year each. She was eighty-two and very frail.

The brothers celebrated the good news with a carouse up in Montmartre. Naturally their chief topic of conversation was how long the old bird would keen on her perch. In any case, it could not be many years. With any luck it might be only a few weeks. The fortune seemed blinding. It would mean comfort and security to the end of their days. The rejoicings were mixed with recriminations against the old man for his stinginess. Why couldn't he have left them a lump sum down now? Why did he want to waste all this good gold on the Church? Why all this trustee business?

There was little they could do but await developments. Except that in the meantime—after a decent interval—they might try and touch the old lady for a bit. They parted, and the next day set about their business in cheerier spirits.

For a time they were extremely tactful. They made formal calls on Aunt Rosalie, inquiring after her health, and offering their services in any capacity whatsoever. But at the end of a month Henri called hurriedly one morning, and after the usual professions of solicitude asked his aunt if she could possibly lend him one hundred and twenty francs to pay the doctor who had attended his wife and baby. She lent him forty, grumbling at his foolishness at having children he could not afford to keep. A week later came Paul with a story about being robbed by a client. He wanted a hundred. She lent him ten.

When these appeals had been repeated three or four times, and received similar treatment—and sometimes no treatment at all—the old lady began to get annoyed. She was becoming more and more eccentric. She now had a companion, an angular, middle-aged woman named Mme Chavanne, who appeared like a protecting goddess. Sometimes when the brothers called, Mme Chavanne would say that Mme Taillandier was too unwell to see anyone. If this news had been true it would have been good news indeed, but the brothers suspected that it was all pre-arranged. Two years went by, and they both began to despair.

'She may live to a hundred,' said Paul.

'We shall die of old age, first,' grumbled Henri.

It was difficult to borrow money on the strength of the will. In the first place their friends were more of the borrowing than the lending class. And, anyone who had a little was suspicious of the story, and wanted all kinds of securities. It was Paul who first thought of going to an insurance company to try to raise money on the reversionary interest. They did succeed in the end in getting an insurance company to advance them two thousand francs each, but the negotiations took five months to complete, and by the time they had insured their lives, paid the lawyer's fees and paid for the various deeds and stamps, and signed some thirty or forty forms, each man only received a little over a thousand francs, which was quickly lost in paying accrued debts and squandering the remainder. Their hopes were raised by the dismissal of Mme Chavanne, only to be lowered again by the arrival of an even more aggressive companion. The companions came and went with startling rapidity. None of them could stand for any time the old lady's eccentricity and ill-temper. The whole of the staff was always being changed. The only one who remained loyal all through was the portly cook, Ernestine. Even this may have been due to the fact that she never came in touch with her mistress. She was an excellent cook, and she never moved from the kitchen. Moreover, the cooking required by Mme Taillandier was of the simplest nature, and she seldom entertained. And, she hardly ever left her apartment. Any complaints that were made were made through the housekeeper, and the complaints and their retaliations became mellowed in the process; for Ernestine also had a temper of her own.

Nearly another year passed before what appeared to Paul to be a mild stroke of good fortune came his way. Things had been going from bad to worse. Neither of the brothers was in a position to lend a sou to the other. Henri's family was becoming a greater drag, and people were not buying Paul's trinkets.

One day, during an interview with his aunt—he had been trying to borrow more money—he fainted in her presence. It is difficult to know what it was about this act which affected the old lady, but she ordered him to be put to bed in one of the rooms of the villa. Possibly, she jumped to the conclusion that he had fainted from lack of food—which was not true, Paul never went without food and drink—and she suddenly realized that after all he was her husband's sister's son. He must certainly have looked pathetic, this white-faced man, well past middle age, and broken in life. Whatever it was, she showed a broad streak of compassion for him. She ordered her servants to look after him, and to allow him to remain until she countermanded the order.

Paul, who had certainly felt faint, but quickly seized the occasion to make it as dramatic as possible, saw in this an opportunity to wheedle his way into his aunt's favours. His behaviour was exemplary. The next morning, looking very white and shaky, he visited her, and asked her to allow him to go, as he had no idea of abusing her hospitality. If he had taken up the opposite attitude she would probably have turned him out, but because he suggested going she ordered him to stop. During the daytime he went about his dubious business, but he continued to return there at night to sleep, and to enjoy a good dinner cooked by the admirable Ernestine. He was in clover.

Henri was naturally envious when he heard of his brother's good fortune. And, Paul was fearful that Henri would spoil the whole game by going and throwing a fit himself in the presence of the aunt. But this, of course, would have been too obvious and foolish for even Henri to consider seriously. And, he racked his brains for some means of inveigling the old lady. Every plan he put forth, however, Paul sat upon. He was quite comfortable himself, and he didn't see the point of his brother butting in.

'Besides,' he said, 'she may turn me out any day. Then you can have your shot.'

They quarrelled about this, and did not see each other for some time. One would have thought that Henri's appeal to Mme Taillandier would have been stronger than Paul's. He was a struggling individual, with a wife and four children. Paul was a notorious ne'er-do-well, and he had no attachments. Nevertheless, the old lady continued to support Paul. Perhaps, it was because he was a big man, and she liked big men. Her husband had been a man of fine physique. Henri was puny, and she despised him. She had never had children of her own, and she disliked children. She was always upbraiding Henri and his wife for their fecundity. Any attempt to pander to her emotions through the sentiment of childhood failed. She would not have the children in her house. And, any small acts of charity which she bestowed upon them seemed to be done more with the idea of giving her an opportunity to inflict her sarcasm and venom upon them than out of kindness of heart.

In Paul, on the other hand, she seemed to find something slightly attractive. She sometimes sent for him, and he, all agog—expecting to get his notice to quit—would be agreeably surprised to find that, on the contrary, she had some little commission she wished him to execute. And, you may rest assured that he never failed to make a few francs out of all these occasions. The notice to quit did not come. It may be—poor deluded woman—that she regarded him as some kind of protection. He was in any case the only 'man' who slept under her roof.

At first she seldom spoke to him, but as time went on she

would sometimes send for him to relieve her loneliness. Nothing could have been more ingratiating than Paul's manners in these knowing circumstances. He talked expansively about politics, beforehand his aunt's views, and just what she would like him to say. Her eyesight was very bad, and he would read her the news of the day, and tell her what was happening in Paris. He humoured her every whim. He was astute enough to see that it would be foolish and dangerous to attempt to borrow money for the moment. He was biding his time, and trying to think out the most profitable plan of campaign. There was no immediate hurry. His bed was comfortable, and Ernestine's cooking was excellent.

In another year's time he had established himself as quite one of the permanent household. He was consulted about the servants, and the doctors, and the management of the house, everything except the control of money, which was jealously guarded by a firm of lawyers. Many a time he would curse his uncle's foresight. The old man's spirit seemed to be hovering in the dim recesses of the over-crowded rooms, mocking him. For the old lady, eccentric and foolish in many ways, kept a strict check upon her dividends. It was her absorbing interest in life, that and an old grey perroquet, which she treated like a child. Its name was Anna, and it used to walk up and down her table at mealtimes and feed off her own plate. Finding himself so firmly entrenched Paul's assurance gradually increased. He began to treat his aunt as an equal, and sometimes even to contradict her, and she did not seem to resent it.

In the meantime, Henri was eating his heart out with jealousy and sullen rage. The whole thing was unfair. He occasionally saw Paul, who boasted openly of his strong position in the Taillandier household, and he would not believe that Paul was not getting money out of the old lady as well as board and lodging. With no additional expenses Paul was better dressed than he used to be, and he looked fatter and better in health. All—or nearly all—of Henri's appeals, although pitched in a most pathetic key, were rebuffed. He felt a bitter hatred against his aunt, his brother, and life in general. If only she would die! What was the good of life to a woman at eighty-five or six? And, there was he—four young children, clamouring for food, and clothes, and the ordinary decent comforts. And, there was Paul, idling his days away at cafés and his nights at cabarets—nothing to do, and no responsibilities.

Meeting Paul one day he said:

'I say, old boy, couldn't you spring me a hundred francs? I haven't the money to pay my rent next week.'

'She gives me nothing,' replied Paul.

Henri did not believe this, but it would be undiplomatic to quarrel. He said:

'Aren't there—isn't there some little thing lying about the villa you could slip in your pocket? We could sell it, see? Go shares. I'm desperately pushed.'

Paul looked down his nose. Name of a pig! Did Henri think he had never thought of that? Many and many a time the temptation had come to him. But no; every few months people came from the lawyer's office, and the inventory of the whole household was checked. The servants could not be suspected. They were not selected without irreproachable characters. If he were suspected—well, all kinds of unpleasant things might crop up. Oh, no, he was too well off where he was. The game was to lie in wait. The old lady simply must die soon. She had even been complaining of her chest that morning. She was always playing with the perroquet. Somehow this bird got on Paul's nerves. He wanted to wring its neck. He imitated the way she would say: 'There's a pretty lady! Oh, my sweet! Another nice grape for my little one. There's a pretty lady!' He told Henri all about this, and the elder brother went on his way with a grunt that only conveyed doubt and suspicion.

In view of this position it seemed strange that in the end it was Paul who was directly responsible for the dénouement in the Taillandier household. His success went to his rather weak head like wine. He began to swagger and buster and abuse his aunt's hospitality. And, curiously enough, the more he advanced the further she withdrew. The eccentric old lady seemed to be losing her powers of resistance so far as he was concerned. And, he began to borrow small sums of money from her, and, as she acquiesced so readily, to increase his demands. He let his travelling business go, and sometimes he would get lost for days at a time. He would spend his time at the races, and drinking with doubtful acquaintances in obscure cafés. Sometimes he won, but in the majority of cases he lost. He ran up bills and got into debt. By cajoling small sums out of his aunt he kept his debtors at bay for nearly nine months.

But one evening he came to see Henri in a great state of distress. His face, which had taken on a healthier glow when he first went to live with his aunt, had become puffy and livid. His eyes were bloodshot.

'Old boy,' he said, 'I'm at my wits' end. I've got to find seven thousand francs by the twenty-first of the month, or they're going to foreclose. How do you stand? I'll pay you back.'

To try to borrow money from Henri was like appealing to the desert for a cooling draught. He also had to find money by the twenty-first, and he was overdrawn at the bank. They exchanged confidences, and in their mutual distress they felt sorry for each other and for themselves. It was a November evening, and the rain was driving along the boulevards in fitful gusts. After trudging a long way they turned into a little café in the Rue de la Roquette, and sat down and ordered two cognacs. The café was almost deserted. A few men in mackintoshes were scattered around reading the evening papers. They sat at a marble table in the corner and tried to think of ways and means. But after a time a silence fell between them. There seemed nothing more to suggest. They could hear the rain beating on the skylight. An old man four tables away was poring over *La Patrie*.

Suddenly, Henri looked furtively around the room and clutched his brother's arm.

'Paul!' he whispered.

'What is it?'

'Do you remember—it has all come back to me—suddenly—one night, a night something like this—it must be give or six years ago—we were seated here in this same café—do you remember?'

'No. I don't remember. What was it?'

'It was the night of that murder in the Landes district. We got talking about—don't you remember?'

Paul scratched his temple and sipped the cognac. Henri leant closer to him.

'You said—you said that if you lived with anyone, it was the easiest thing in the world to murder them. An accident, you know. And, you go screaming into the street—'

Paul started, and stared at his brother, who continued:

'You said that if ever you—you had to do it, you would guarantee that you would take every trouble. You wouldn't leave a trace behind.'

Paul was acting. He pretended to half-remember, to half-understand. But his eyes narrowed. Imbecile! Hadn't he been through it all in imagination a hundred times? Hadn't he already been planning and scheming an act for which his brother would reap half the benefit? Nevertheless, he was staggered. He never imagined that the suggestion would come from Henri. He was secretly relieved. If Henri was to receive half the benefit, let him also share half the responsibilities. The risk in any case would be wholly his. He grinned enigmatically, and they put their heads together. And so, in that dim corner of the café was planned the perfect murder.

Coining up against the actual proposition, Paul had long since realized that the affair was not so easy of accomplishment as he had so airily suggested. For the thing must be done without violence, without clues, without a trace. Such ideas as leaving the window open at night were out of the question, as the companion slept in the same room. Moreover, the old lady was quite capable of getting out of bed and shutting it herself if she felt a draught. Some kind of accident? Yes, but what? Suppose she slipped and broke her neck when Paul was in the room. It would be altogether too suspicious. Besides, she would probably only partially break her neck. She would regain sufficient consciousness to tell. To drown her in her bath? The door was always locked or the companion hovering around.

'You've always got to remember,' whispered Paul, 'if any suspicion falls on me, there's the motive. There's strong motive why I should—it's got to be absolutely untraceable. I don't care if some people do suspect afterwards—when we've got the money.'

'What about her food?'

'The food is cooked by Ernestine, and the companion serves

it. Besides, suppose I got a chance to tamper with the food, how am I going to get hold of—you know?'

'Weed-killer?'

'Yes, I should be in a pretty position if they traced the fact that I had bought weed-killer. You might buy some and let me have a little on the quiet.

Henri turned pale. 'No, no; the motive applies to me, too. They'd get us both.'

When the two pleasant gentlemen parted at midnight their plans were still very immature, but they arranged to meet the following evening. It was the thirteenth of the month. To save the situation the deed must be accomplished within eight days. Of course, they wouldn't get the money at once, but, knowing the circumstances, creditors would be willing to wait. When they met the following evening in the Café des Sentiers, Paul appeared flushed and excited, and Henri was pale and on edge. He hadn't slept. He wanted to wash the whole thing out.

'And, sell up your home, I suppose?' sneered Paul.

'Listen, my little cabbage. I've got it. Don't distress yourself. You proposed this last night. I've been thinking about it and watching for months. Ernestine is a good cook, and very methodical. Oh, very methodical! She does everything every day in the same way exactly to schedule. My apartment is on the same floor, so I am able to appreciate her punctuality and exactness. The old woman eats sparingly and according to routine. One night she has fish. The next night she has a soufflé made with two eggs. Fish, soufflé, fish, soufflé, regular as the beat of a clock. Now, listen. After lunch every day Ernestine washes up the plates and pans. After that she prepares roughly the evening meal. If it is a fish night, she prepares the fish ready to pop into the pan. If it is a soufflé night, she beats up two eggs and puts them ready in a basin. Having done that, she changes her frock, powders her nose, and goes over to the convent to see her sister who is working there. She is away an hour and a half. She returns punctually at four o'clock. You could set your watch by her movements.'

'Yes, but—'

'It is difficult to insert what I propose in fish, but I don't see any difficulty in dropping it into two beaten-up eggs, and giving an extra twist to the egg-whisk, or whatever they call it.'

Henri's face was quite grey.

'But—but—Paul, how are you going to get hold of the poison?'

'Who said anything about poison?'

'Well, but what?'

'That's where you come in.'

'Yes, you're in it, too, aren't you? You get half the spoils, don't you? Why shouldn't you—some time tomorrow when your wife's out—'

'What?'

'Just grind up a piece of glass.'

'Glass!'

'Yes, you've heard of glass, haven't you? An ordinary piece of broken wine-glass will do. Grind it up as fine as a powder, the finer the better, the finer the more-effective.'

Henri gasped. No, no, he couldn't do this thing. Very well, then; if he was such a coward Paul would have to do it himself. And perhaps, when the time came Henri would also be too frightened to draw his dividends. Perhaps, he would like to make them over to his dear brother Paul? Come, it was only a little thing to do. Eight days to the twenty-first. Tomorrow, fish day, but Wednesday would be soufflé. So easy, so untraceable, so safe.

'But you,' whined Henri, 'they will suspect you.'

'Even if they do they can prove nothing. But in order to avoid this unpleasantness I propose to leave home soon after breakfast. I shall return at a quarter-past three, letting myself in through the stable yard. The stables, as you know, are not used. There is no one else on that floor. Ernestine is upstairs. She only comes down to answer the front-door bell. I shall be in and out of the house within five minutes, and I shan't return till late at night, when perhaps—I may be too late to render assistance.'

Henri was terribly agitated. On one hand was—just murder, a thing he had never connected himself within his life. On the other hand was comfort for himself and his family, an experience he had given up hoping for. It was in any case not exactly murder on his part. It was Paul's murder. At the same time, knowing all about it, being an accessory before the fact, it would seem contemptible to a degree to put the whole onus on Paul. Grinding up a piece of glass was such a little thing. It couldn't possibly incriminate him. Nobody could ever prove that he'd done it. But it was a terrible step to take.

'Have another cognac, my little cabbage.'

It was Paul's voice that jerked him back to actuality. He said: 'All right, yes, yes,' but whether this referred to the cognac or to the act of grinding up a piece of glass he hardly knew himself.

From that moment to twenty-four hours later, when he handed over a white packet to his brother across the same table at the Café des Sentiers, Henri seemed to be in a nightmarish dream. He had no recollection of how he had passed the time. He seemed to pass from that last cognac to this one, and the interval was a blank.

'Fish today, soufflé tomorrow,' he heard Paul chuckling.

'Brother, you have done your work well.'

When Paul went he wanted to call after him to come back, but he was frightened of the sound of his own voice. He was terribly frightened. He went to bed very late and could not sleep. The next morning he awoke with a headache, and he got his wife to telegraph to the office to say that he was too ill to come. He lay in bed all day, visualizing over and over and over again the possible events of the evening.

Paul would be caught. Someone would catch him actually putting the powder into the eggs. He would be arrested. Paul would give him away. Why did Paul say it was so easy to murder anyone if you lived with them? It wasn't easy at all. The whole thing was chock-a-block with dangers and pitfalls. Pitfalls! At half-past three he started up in bed. He had a vision of himself and Paul being guillotined side by side! He must stop it at any cost. He began to get up. Then he realized that it was already too late. The deed had been done. Paul had said that he would be in and out of the house within five minutes at three-fifteen—a quarter of an hour ago! Where was Paul? Would he be coming to see him? He was going to spend the evening out somewhere, 'returning late at night'.

He dressed feverishly. There was still time. He could call at his aunt's. Rush down to the kitchen, seize the basin of beaten-up eggs, and throw them away. But where? How? By the time he got there Ernestine would have returned. She would want to know all about it. The egg mixture would be examined, analysed. God in Heaven! It was too late! The thing would have to go on, and he suffer and wait.

Having dressed, he went out after saying to his wife: 'It's all right. It's going to be all right,' not exactly knowing what he meant. He walked rapidly along the streets with no fixed destination in his mind. He found himself in the Café Rue de la Roquette, where the idea was first conceived, where he had reminded his brother.

He sat there drinking, waiting for the hours to pass.

Soufflé day, and the old lady dined at seven! It was now not quite five. He hoped Paul would turn up. A stranger tried to engage him in conversation. The stranger apparently had some grievance against a railway company. He wanted to tell him all the details about a contract for rivets, over which he had been disappointed. Henri didn't understand a word he was talking about. He didn't listen. He wanted the stranger to drop down dead or vanish into thin air. At last he called the waiter and paid for his reckoning, indicated by a small pile of saucers. From there he walked rapidly to the Café des Sentiers, looking for Paul. He was not there. Six o'clock. One hour more. He could not keep still. He paid and went on again, calling at café after café. A quarter to seven. Pray God that she threw it away. Had he ground it fine enough?

Five minutes to seven. Seven o'clock. Now. He picked up his hat and went again. The brandy had gone to his head. At half-past seven he laughed recklessly. After all, what was the good of life to this old woman of eighty-six? He tried to convince himself that he had done it for the sake of his wife and children. He tried to concentrate on the future, how he could manage on eight or ten thousand francs a year. He would give notice at the office, be rude to people who had been bullying him for years—that old blackguard Mocquin!

At ten o'clock he was drunk, torpid, and indifferent. The whole thing was over for good or ill. What did it matter? He terribly wanted to see Paul, but he was too tired to care very much. The irrevocable step had been taken. He went home to bed and fell into a heavy drunken sleep.

'Henri! Henri, wake up! What is the matter with you?' His wife was shaking him. He blinked his way into a partial condition of consciousness. November sunlight was pouring into the room.

'It's late, isn't it?' he said, involuntarily.

'It's past eight. You'll be late at the office. You didn't go yesterday. If you go on like this you'll get the sack, and then what shall we do?'

Slowly the recollection of last night's events came back to him.

'There's nothing to worry about,' he said. 'I'm too ill to go today. Send them another telegram. It'll be all right.'

His wife looked at him searchingly. 'You've been drinking,' she said. 'Oh, you men! God knows what will become of us.'

She appeared to be weeping in her apron. It struck him forcibly at that instant how provoking and small women are. Here was Jeannette crying over her petty troubles. Whereas he—

The whole thing was becoming vivid again. Where was Paul? What had happened? Was it at all likely that he could go down to an office on a day like this, a day that was to decide his fate?

He groaned, and elaborated rather pathetically his imaginary ailments, anything to keep this woman quiet. She left him at last, and he lay there waiting for something to happen. The hours passed. What would be the first intimation? Paul or the gendarmes? Thoughts of the latter stirred him to a state of fevered activity. About midday he arose, dressed, and went out. He told his wife he was going to the office, but he had no intention of doing so. He went and drank coffee at a place up in the Marais. He was terrified of his old haunts. He wandered from place to place, uncertain how to act. Late in the afternoon he entered a café in the Rue Alibert. At a kiosk outside he bought a late edition of an afternoon newspaper. He sat down, ordered a drink and opened the newspaper. He glanced at the central news page, and as his eye absorbed one paragraph he unconsciously uttered a low scream. The paragraph was as follows:

> Mysterious Affair at Chantilly
>
> A mysterious affair occurred at Chantilly this morning. A middle-aged man, named Paul Denoyel, complained of pains in the stomach after eating an omelette. He died soon after in great agony. He was staying with his aunt, Mme Taillandier. No other members of the household were affected. The matter is to be inquired into.

The rest was a dream. He was only vaguely conscious of the events which followed. He wandered through it all, the instinct of self-preservation bidding him hold his tongue in all circumstances. He knew nothing. He had seen nothing. He had a visionary recollection of a plump, weeping Ernestine, at the inquest, enlarging upon the eccentricities of her mistress. A queer woman, who would brook no contradiction. He heard a lot about the fish day and the soufflé day, and how the old lady insisted that this was a fish day, and, and that she had had a soufflé the day before. You could not argue with her when she was like that. And, Ernestine had beaten up the eggs all ready for the soufflé-most provoking! But Ernestine was a good cook, of method and economy. She wasted nothing. What should she do with the eggs? Why, of course, Mr Paul, who since he had come to live there was never content with a *café cornplet*. He must have a breakfast, like these English and other foreigners do. She made him an omelette, which he ate heartily.

Then the beaten-up eggs with their deadly mixture were intended for Mme Taillandier? But who was responsible for this? Ernestine? But there was no motive here. Ernestine gained nothing by her mistress's death. Indeed she only stood to lose her situation. The inquiry went on a long while. Henri himself was conscious of being in the witness-box. He knew nothing. He couldn't understand it. His brother would not be likely to do that. He himself was prostrate with grief. He loved his brother.

There was nothing to do but return an open verdict. Shadowy figures passed before his mind's eye—shadowy figures and shadowy realizations. He had perfectly murdered his brother. The whole of the dividends of the estate would one day be his, and his wife's and children's. Eighteen thousand francs a year! One day—

One vision more vivid than the rest—the old lady on the day following the inquest, seated bolt upright at her table, like a figure of perpetuity, playing with the old grey perroquet, stroking its mangy neck.

'There's a pretty lady! Oh, my sweet! Another nice grape for my little one. There's a pretty lady!'

THE RED-HEADED LEAGUE

Arthur Conan Doyle

I had called upon my friend, Mr Sherlock Holmes, one day in the autumn of last year, and found him in deep conversation with a very stout, florid-faced elderly gentleman, with fiery red hair. With an apology for my intrusion, I was about to withdraw, when Holmes pulled me abruptly into the room and closed the door behind me.

'You could not possibly have come at a better time, my dear Watson,' he said, cordially.

'I was afraid that you were engaged.'

'So I am. Very much so.'

'Then I can wait in the next room.'

'Not at all. This gentleman, Mr Wilson, has been my partner and helper in many of my most successful cases, and I have no doubt that he will be of the utmost use to me in yours also.'

The stout gentleman half rose from his chair and gave a bob of greeting, with a quick little questioning glance from his small, fat-encircled eyes.

'Try the settee,' said Holmes, relapsing into his armchair, and putting his finger tips together, as was his custom when in judicial moods. 'I know, my dear Watson, that you share my love of all that is bizarre and outside the conventions and humdrum routine of everyday life. You have shown your relish for it by the enthusiasm which has prompted you to chronicle, and, if you will excuse my saying so, somewhat to embellish so many of my own little adventures.'

'Your cases have indeed been of the greatest interest to me,' I observed.

'You will remember that I remarked the other day, just before we went into the very simple problem presented by Miss Mary Sutherland, that for strange effects and extraordinary combinations we must go to life itself, which is always far more daring than any effort of the imagination.'

'A proposition which I took the liberty of doubting.'

2

'You did, doctor, but none the less you must come round to my view, for otherwise I shall keep on piling fact upon fact on you, until your reason breaks down under them and acknowledge me to be right. Now, Mr Jabez Wilson here has been good enough to call upon me this morning, and to begin a narrative which promises to be one of the most singular which I have listened to for some time. You have heard me remark that the strangest and most unique things are very often connected not with the larger but with the smaller crimes, and occasionally, indeed, where there is room for doubt whether any positive crime has been committed. As far as I have heard, it is impossible for me to say whether the present case is an instance of crime or not, but the course of events is certainly among the most singular that I have ever listened to. Perhaps, Mr Wilson, you would have the great kindness to recommence your narrative. I ask you, not merely because my friend, Dr Watson, has not heard the opening part, but also because the peculiar nature of the story makes me anxious to have every possible detail from your lips. As a rule, when I have heard some slight indication of the course of events I am able to guide myself by the thousands of other similar cases which occur to my memory. In the present instance I am forced to admit that the facts are, to the best of my belief, unique.'

The portly client puffed out his chest with an appearance of some little pride, and pulled a dirty and wrinkled newspaper from the inside pocket of his greatcoat. As he glanced down the advertisement column, with his head thrust forward, and the paper flattened out upon his knee, I took a good look at the man, and endeavoured, after the fashion of my companion, to read the indications which might be presented by his dress or appearance.

I did not gain very much, however, by my inspection. Our visitor bore every mark of being an average commonplace British tradesman, obese, pompous, and slow. He wore rather baggy grey shepherd's check trousers, a not over-clean black frock coat, unbuttoned in the front, and a drab waistcoat with a heavy brassy Albert chain, and a square pierced bit of metal dangling down as an ornament. A frayed top hat and a faded brown overcoat with a wrinkled velvet collar lay upon a chair beside him. Altogether, look as I would, there was nothing remarkable about the man save his blazing red head and the expression of extreme chagrin and discontent upon his features.

3

Sherlock Holmes's quick eye took in my occupation, and he shook his head with a smile as he noticed my questioning glances. 'Beyond the obvious facts that he has at some time done manual labour, that he takes snuff, that he is a Freemason, that he has been in China, and that he has done a considerable amount of writing lately, I can deduce nothing else.'

Mr Jabez Wilson started up in his chair, with his forefinger upon the paper, but his eyes upon my companion.

'How, in the name of good fortune, did you know all that, Mr Holmes?' he asked. 'How did you know, for example, that I did manual labour? It's as true as gospel, for I began as a ship's carpenter.'

'Your hands, my dear sir. Your right hand is quite a size larger than your left. You have worked with it and the muscles are more developed.'

'Well, the snuff, then, and the Freemasonry?'

'I won't insult your intelligence by telling you how I read that, especially as, rather against the strict rules of your order, you use an arc and compass breastpin.'

'Ah, of course, I forgot that. But the writing?'

'What else can be indicated by that right cuff so very shiny for five inches, and the left one with the smooth patch near the elbow where you rest it upon the desk.'

'Well, but China?'

'The fish which you have tattooed immediately above your wrist could only have been done in China. I have made a small study of tattoo marks, and have even contributed to the literature of the subject. That trick of staining the fishes' scales of a delicate pink is quite peculiar to China. When, in addition, I see a Chinese coin hanging from your watch chain, the matter becomes even more simple.'

Mr Jabez Wilson laughed heavily. 'Well, I never!' said he. 'I thought at first that you had done something clever, but I see that there was nothing in it after all.'

'I begin to think, Watson,' said Holmes, 'that I make a mistake in explaining. "Omne ignotom pro magnifico," you know, and my poor little reputation, such as it is, will suffer shipwreck if I am so candid. Can you not find the advertisement, Mr Wilson?'

'Yes, I have got it now,' he answered, with his thick, red finger planted halfway down the column. 'Here it is. This is what began it all. You just read it for yourself, sir.'

I took the paper from him and read as follows:

'TO THE RED-HEADED LEAGUE: On account of the bequest of the late Ezekiah Hopkins, of Lebanon, Pa., U. S. A., there is now another vacancy open which entitles a member of the League to a salary of four pounds a week for purely nominal services. All red-headed men who are sound in body and mind and above the age of twenty-one years are eligible. Apply in person on Monday, at eleven o'clock, to Duncan Ross, at the offices of the League, 7 Pope's Court, Fleet Street.'

'What on earth does this mean?' I ejaculated, after I had twice read over the extraordinary announcement.

Holmes chuckled and wriggled in his chair, as was his habit when in high spirits. 'It is a little off the beaten track, isn't it?' said he. 'And now, Mr Wilson, off you go at scratch, and tell us all about yourself, your household, and the effect which this advertisement had upon your fortunes. You will first make a note, doctor, of the paper and the date.'

'It is *The Morning Chronicle* of 27 April 1890. Just two months ago.'

'Very good. Now, Mr Wilson.'

5

'Well, it is just as I have been telling you, Mr Sherlock Holmes,' said Jabez Wilson, mopping his forehead, 'I have a small pawnbroker's business at Saxe-Coburg Square, near the City. It's not a very large affair, and of late years it has not done more than just give me a living. I used to be able to keep two assistants, but now I only keep one; and I would have a job to pay him but that he is willing to come for half wages, so as to learn the business.'

'What is the name of this obliging youth?' asked Sherlock Holmes.

'His name is Vincent Spaulding, and he's not such a youth either. It's hard to say his age. I should not wish a smarter assistant, Mr Holmes; and I know very well that he could better himself, and earn twice what I am able to give him. But, after all, if he is satisfied, why should I put ideas in his head?'

'Why, indeed? You seem most fortunate in having an employee who comes under the full market price. It is not a common experience among employers in this age. I did't know that your assistant is not as remarkable as your advertisement.'

'Oh, he has his faults, too,' said Mr Wilson. 'Never was such a fellow for photography. Snapping away with a camera when he ought to be improving his mind, and then diving down into the cellar like a rabbit into its hole to develop his pictures. That is his main fault; but, on the whole, he's a good worker. There's no vice in him.'

'He is still with you, I presume?'

'Yes, sir. He and a girl of fourteen, who does a bit of simple cooking, and keeps the place clean—that's all I have in the house, for I am a widower, and never had any family. We live very quietly, sir, the three of us; and we keep a roof over our heads, and pay our debts, if we do nothing more.

6

'The first thing that put us out was that advertisement. Spaulding, he came down into the office just this day eight weeks, with this very paper in his hand, and he says:

'"I wish to the Lord, Mr Wilson, that I was a red-headed man."

'"Why that?" I asks.

'"Why," says he, 'here's another vacancy on the League of the Red-headed Men. It's worth quite a little fortune to any man who gets it, and I understand that there are more vacancies than there are men, so that the trustees are at their wits' end what to do with the money. If my hair would only change colour here's a nice little crib all ready for me to step into."

'Why, what is it, then?' I asked. 'You see, Mr Holmes, I am a very stay-at-home man, and, as my business came to me instead of my having to go to it, I was often weeks on end without putting my foot over the doormat. In that way I didn't know much of what was going on outside, and I was always glad of a bit of news.'

'Have you never heard of the League of the Red-headed Men?' he asked, with his eyes open.

'Never.'

'Why, I wonder at that, for you are eligible yourself for one of the vacancies.'

'And what are they worth?' I asked.

'Oh, merely a couple of hundred a year, but the work is slight, and it need not interfere very much with one's other occupations.'

'Well, you can easily think that that made me prick up my ears, for the business has not been very good for some years, and an extra couple of hundred would have been very handy.

'Tell me all about it,' said I.

7

'Well,' said he, showing me the advertisement, 'you can see for yourself that the League has a vacancy, and there is the address where you should apply for particulars. As far as I can make out, the League was founded by an American millionaire, Ezekiah Hopkins, who was very peculiar in his ways. He was himself red-headed, and he had a great sympathy for all red-headed men; so, when he died, it was found that he had left his enormous fortune in the hands of trustees, with instructions to apply the interest to the providing of easy berths to men whose hair is of that colour. From all I hear it is splendid pay, and very little to do.'

'But,' said I, 'there would be millions of red-headed men who would apply.'

'Not so many as you might think,' he answered. 'You see it is really confined to Londoners, and to grown men. This American had started from London when he was young, and he wanted to do the old town a good turn. Then, again, I have heard it is of no use your applying if your hair is light red, or dark red, or anything but real, bright, blazing, fiery red. Now, if you cared to apply, Mr Wilson, you would just walk in; but perhaps it would hardly be worth your while to put yourself out of the way for the sake of a few hundred pounds.'

'Now it is a fact, gentlemen, as you may see for yourselves, that my hair is of a very full and rich tint, so that it seemed to me that, if there was to be any competition in the matter,

I stood as good a chance as any man that I had ever met. Vincent Spaulding seemed to know so much about it that I thought he might prove useful, so I just ordered him to put up the shutters for the day, and to come right away with me. He was very willing to have a holiday, so we shut the business up, and started off for the address that was given to us in the advertisement.'

8

'I never hope to see such a sight as that again, Mr Holmes. From north, south, east, and west every man who had a shade of red in his hair had tramped into the City to answer the advertisement. Fleet Street was choked with red-headed folk, and Pope's Court looked like a coster's orange barrow. I should not have thought there were so many in the whole country as were brought together by that single advertisement. Every shade of colour they were—straw, lemon, orange, brick, Irish setter, liver, clay; but, as Spaulding said, there were not many who had the real vivid flame-coloured tint. When I saw how many were waiting, I would have given it up in despair; but Spaulding would not hear of it. How he did it I could not imagine, but he pushed and pulled and butted until he got me through the crowd, and right up to the steps which led to the office. There was a double stream upon the stair, some going up in hope, and some coming back dejected; but we wedged in as well as we could, and soon found ourselves in the office.'

'Your experience has been a most entertaining one,' remarked Holmes, as his client paused and refreshed his memory with a huge pinch of snuff. 'Pray continue your very interesting statement.'

'There was nothing in the office but a couple of wooden

chairs and a deal table, behind which sat a small man, with a head that was even redder than mine. He said a few words to each candidate as he came up, and then he always managed to find some fault in them which would disqualify them. Getting a vacancy did not seem to be such a very easy matter after all. However, when our turn came, the little man was much more favourable to me than to any of the others, and he closed the door as we entered, so that he might have a private word with us.

'This is Mr Jabez Wilson,' said my assistant, 'and he is willing to fill a vacancy in the League.'

9

'And he is admirably suited for it,' the other answered. 'He has every requirement. I cannot recall when I have seen anything so fine.' He took a step backward, cocked his head on one side, and gazed at my hair until I felt quite bashful. Then suddenly he plunged forward, wrung my hand, and congratulated me warmly on my success.

'It would be injustice to hesitate,' said he. 'You will, however, I am sure, excuse me for taking an obvious precaution.' With that he seized my hair in both his hands, and tugged until I yelled with the pain. 'There is water in your eyes,' said he, as he released me. 'I perceive that all is as it should be. But we have to be careful, for we have twice been deceived by wigs and once by paint. I could tell you tales of cobbler's wax which would disgust you with human nature.' He stepped over to the window and shouted through it at the top of his voice that the vacancy was filled. A groan of disappointment came up from below, and the folk all trooped away in different directions, until there was not a red head to be seen except my own and that of the manager.

'My name,' said he, 'is Mr Duncan Ross, and I am myself one of the pensioners upon the fund left by our noble benefactor. Are you a married man, Mr Wilson? Have you a family?'

'I answered that I had not.

'His face fell immediately.

'Dear me!' he said, gravely, 'that is very serious indeed! I am sorry to hear you say that. The fund was, of course, for the propagation and spread of the red heads as well as for their maintenance. It is exceedingly unfortunate that you should be a bachelor.'

'My face lengthened at this, Mr Holmes, for I thought that I was not to have the vacancy after all; but, after thinking it over for a few minutes, he said that it would be all right.'

10

'In the case of another,' said he, 'the objection might be fatal, but we must stretch a point in favour of a man with such a head of hair as yours. When shall you be able to enter upon your new duties?'

'Well, it is a little awkward, for I have a business already,' said I.

'Oh, never mind about that, Mr Wilson!' said Vincent Spaulding. 'I shall be able to look after that for you.'

'What would be the hours?' I asked.

'Ten to two.'

'Now a pawnbroker's business is mostly done of an evening, Mr Holmes, especially Thursday and Friday evenings, which is just before pay day; so it would suit me very well to earn a little in the mornings. Besides, I knew that my assistant was a good man, and that he would see to anything that turned up.

'That would suit me very well,' said I. 'And the pay?'

'Is four pounds a week.'

'And the work?'

'Is purely nominal.'

'What do you call purely nominal?'

'Well, you have to be in the office, or at least in the building, the whole time. If you leave, you forfeit your whole position forever. The will is very clear upon that point. You don't comply with the conditions if you budge from the office during that time.'

'It's only four hours a day, and I should not think of leaving,' said I.

'No excuse will avail,' said Mr Duncan Ross, 'neither sickness, nor business, nor anything else. There you must stay, or you lose your billet.'

'And the work?'

11

'Is to copy out the *Encyclopaedia Britannica*. There is the first volume of it in that press. You must find your own ink, pens, and blotting paper, but we provide this table and chair. Will you be ready tomorrow?'

'Certainly,' I answered.

'Then, goodbye, Mr Jabez Wilson, and let me congratulate you once more on the important position which you have been fortunate enough to gain.' He bowed me out of the room, and I went home with my assistant hardly knowing what to say or do, I was so pleased at my own good fortune.

'Well, I thought over the matter all day, and by evening I was in low spirits again; for I had quite persuaded myself that the whole affair must be some great hoax or fraud, though what its object might be I could not imagine. It seemed altogether past belief that anyone could make such a will, or that they would pay such a sum for doing anything so simple as copying out the *Encyclopaedia Britannica*. Vincent Spaulding did what he could to cheer me up, but by bed time I had reasoned myself out of the whole thing. However, in the morning I determined to have a look at it anyhow, so I bought a penny bottle of ink, and with a quill pen and seven sheets of foolscap paper I started off for Pope's Court.

'Well, to my surprise and delight everything was as right as possible. The table was set out ready for me, and Mr Duncan Ross was there to see that I got fairly to work. He started me off upon the letter A, and then he left me; but he would drop in from time to time to see that all was right with me. At two o'clock he bade me good-day, complimented me upon the amount that I had written, and locked the door of the office after me.

'This went on day after day, Mr Holmes, and on Saturday the manager came in and planked down four golden sovereigns for my week's work. It was the same next week, and the same the week after. Every morning I was there at ten, and every afternoon I left at two. By degrees Mr Duncan Ross took to coming in only once of a morning, and then, after a time, he did not come in at all. Still, of course, I never dared to leave the room for an instant, for I was not sure when he might come, and the billet was such a good one, and suited me so well, that I would not risk the loss of it.

12

'Eight weeks passed away like this, and I had written about Abbots, and Archery, and Armor, and Architecture, and Attica, and hoped with diligence that I might get on to the Bs before very long. It cost me something in foolscap, and I had pretty nearly filled a shelf with my writings. And then suddenly the whole business came to an end.'

'To an end?'

'Yes, sir. And no later than this morning. I went to my work as usual at ten o'clock, but the door was shut and locked, with a little square of cardboard hammered onto the middle of the panel with a tack. Here it is, and you can read for yourself.'

He held up a piece of white cardboard, about the size of a sheet of note paper. It read in this fashion:

'THE RED-HEADED LEAGUE IS DISSOLVED.
9 Oct. 1890.'

Sherlock Holmes and I surveyed this curt announcement and the rueful face behind it, until the comical side of the affair so completely overtopped every consideration that we both burst out into a roar of laughter.

'I cannot see that there is anything very funny,' cried our client, flushing up to the roots of his flaming head. 'If you can do nothing better than laugh at me, I can go elsewhere.'

'No, no,' cried Holmes, shoving him back into the chair from which he had half-risen. 'I really wouldn't miss your case for the world. It is most refreshingly unusual. But there is, if you will excuse my saying so, something just a little funny about it. Pray what steps did you take when you found the card upon the door?'

'I was staggered, sir. I did not know what to do. Then I called at the offices around, but none of them seemed to know anything about it. Finally, I went to the landlord, who is an accountant living on the ground floor, and I asked him if he could tell me what had become of the Red-headed League. He said that he had never heard of any such body. Then I asked him who Mr Duncan Ross was. He answered that the name was new to him.'

13

'Well,' said I, 'the gentleman at No. 4.'

'What, the red-headed man?'

'Yes.'

'Oh,' said he, 'his name was William Morris. He was a solicitor, and was using my room as a temporary convenience until his new premises were ready. He moved out yesterday.'

'Where could I find him?'

'Oh, at his new offices. He did tell me the address. Yes, 17 King Edward Street, near St. Paul's.'

'I started off, Mr Holmes, but when I got to that address it was a manufactory of artificial knee-caps, and no one in it had ever heard of either Mr William Morris or Mr Duncan Ross.'

'And what did you do then?' asked Holmes.

'I went home to Saxe-Coburg Square, and I took the advice of my assistant. But he could not help me in any way. He could only say that if I waited I should hear by post. But that was not quite good enough, Mr Holmes. I did not wish to lose such a place without a struggle, so, as I had heard that you were good enough to give advice to poor folk who were in need of it, I came right away to you.'

'And you did very wisely,' said Holmes. 'Your case is an exceedingly remarkable one, and I shall be happy to look into it. From what you have told me I think that it is possible that graver issues hang from it than might at first sight appear.'

'Grave enough!' said Mr Jabez Wilson. 'Why, I have lost four pound a week.'

'As far as you are personally concerned,' remarked Holmes, 'I do not see that you have any grievance against this extraordinary league. On the contrary, you are, as I understand, richer by some thirty pounds, to say nothing of the minute knowledge which you have gained on every subject which comes under the letter A. You have lost nothing by them.'

14

'No, sir. But I want to find out about them, and who they are, and what their object was in playing this prank—if it was a prank—upon me. It was a pretty expensive joke for them, for it cost them two-and-thirty pounds.'

'We shall endeavour to clear up these points for you. And, first, one or two questions, Mr Wilson. This assistant of yours who first called your attention to the advertisement—how long had he been with you?'

'About a month then.'

'How did he come?'

'In answer to an advertisement.'

'Was he the only applicant?'

'No, I had a dozen.'

'Why did you pick him?'

'Because he was handy and would come cheap.'

'At half wages, in fact.'

'Yes.'

'What is he like, this Vincent Spaulding?'

'Small, stout-built, very quick in his ways, no hair on his face, though he's not short of thirty. Has a white splash of acid upon his forehead.'

Holmes sat up in his chair in considerable excitement. 'I thought as much,' said he. 'Have you ever observed that his ears are pierced for earrings?'

'Yes, sir. He told me that a gypsy had done it for him when he was a lad.'

'Hum!' said Holmes, sinking back in deep thought. 'He is still with you?'

'Oh, yes, sir; I have only just left him.'

'And has your business been attended to in your absence?'

15

'Nothing to complain of, sir. There's never very much to do of a morning.'

'That will do, Mr Wilson. I shall be happy to give you an opinion upon the subject in the course of a day or two. Today is Saturday, and I hope that by Monday we may come to a conclusion.'

'Well, Watson,' said Holmes, when our visitor had left us, 'what do you make of it all?'

'I make nothing of it,' I answered frankly. 'It is a most mysterious business.'

'As a rule,' said Holmes, 'the more bizarre a thing is the less mysterious it proves to be. It is your commonplace, featureless crimes which are really puzzling, just as a commonplace face is the most difficult to identify. But I must be prompt over this matter.'

'What are you going to do, then?' I asked.

'To smoke,' he answered. 'It is quite a three-pipe problem, and I beg that you won't speak to me for fifty minutes.' He curled himself up in his chair, with his thin knees drawn up to his hawk-like nose, and there he sat with his eyes closed and his black clay pipe thrusting out like the bill of some strange bird. I had come to the conclusion that he had dropped asleep, and indeed was nodding myself, when he suddenly sprang out of his chair with the gesture of a man who has made up his mind, and put his pipe down upon the mantelpiece.

'Sarasate plays at St. James's Hall this afternoon,' he remarked. 'What do you think, Watson? Could your patients spare you for a few hours?'

'I have nothing to do today. My practice is never very absorbing.'

'Then put on your hat and come. I am going through the City first, and we can have some lunch on the way. I observe that there is a good deal of German music on the programme, which is rather more to my taste than Italian or French. It is introspective, and I want to introspect. Come along!'

16

We travelled by the Underground as far as Aldersgate; and a short walk took us to Saxe-Coburg Square, the scene of the singular story which we had listened to in the morning. It was a poky, little, shabby-genteel place, where four lines of dingy, two-storied brick houses looked out into a small railed-in inclosure, where a lawn of weedy grass, and a few clumps of faded laurel bushes made a hard fight against a smoke-laden and uncongenial atmosphere. Three gilt balls and a brown board with JABEZ WILSON in white letters, upon a corner house, announced the place where our red-headed client carried on his business. Sherlock Holmes stopped in front of it with his head on one side, and looked it all over, with his eyes shining brightly between puckered lids. Then he walked slowly up the street, and then down again to the corner, still looking keenly at the houses. Finally he returned to the pawnbroker's and, having thumped vigorously upon the pavement with his stick two or three times, he went up to the door and knocked. It was instantly opened by a bright-looking, clean-shaven young fellow, who asked him to step in.

'Thank you,' said Holmes, 'I only wished to ask you how you would go from here to the Strand.'

'Third right, fourth left,' answered the assistant, promptly, closing the door.

'Smart fellow, that,' observed Holmes as we walked away. 'He is, in my judgment, the fourth smartest man in London, and for daring I am not sure that he has not a claim to be third. I have known something of him before.'

'Evidently,' said I, 'Mr Wilson's assistant counts for a good deal in this mystery of the Red-headed League. I am sure that you inquired your way merely in order that you might see him.'

'Not him.'

'What then?'

'The knees of his trousers.'

17

'And what did you see?'

'What I expected to see.'

'Why did you beat the pavement?'

'My dear doctor, this is a time for observation, not for talk. We are spies in an enemy's country. We know something of Saxe-Coburg Square. Let us now explore the parts which lie behind it.'

The road in which we found ourselves as we turned round the corner from the retired Saxe-Coburg Square presented as great a contrast to it as the front of a picture does to the back. It was one of the main arteries which convey the traffic of the City to the north and west. The roadway was blocked with the immense stream of commerce flowing in a double tide inward and outward, while the footpaths were black with the hurrying swarm of pedestrians. It was difficult to realize, as we looked at the line of fine shops and stately business premises, that they really abutted on the other side upon the faded and stagnant square which we had just quitted.

'Let me see,' said Holmes, standing at the corner, and glancing along the line, 'I should like just to remember the order of the houses here. It is a hobby of mine to have an exact knowledge of London. There is Mortimer's, the tobacconist; the little newspaper shop, the Coburg branch of the City and Suburban Bank, the Vegetarian Restaurant, and McFarlane's carriage-building depot. That carries us right on to the other block. And now, doctor, we've done our work, so it's time we had some play. A sandwich and a cup of coffee, and then off to violin-land, where all is sweetness, and delicacy, and harmony, and there are no red-headed clients to vex us with their conundrums.'

My friend was an enthusiastic musician, being himself not only a very capable performer, but a composer of no ordinary merit. All the afternoon he sat in the stalls wrapped in the most perfect happiness, gently waving his long thin fingers in time to the music, while his gently smiling face and his languid, dreamy eyes were as unlike those of Holmes the sleuth-hound, Holmes the relentless, keen-witted, ready-handed criminal agent, as it was possible to conceive. In his singular character the dual nature alternately asserted itself, and his extreme exactness and astuteness represented, as I have often thought, the reaction against the poetic and contemplative mood which occasionally predominated in him. The swing of his nature took him from extreme languor to devouring energy; and, as I knew well, he was never so truly formidable as when, for days on end, he had been lounging in his armchair amid his improvisations and his black-letter editions. Then it was that the lust of the chase would suddenly come upon him, and that his brilliant reasoning power would rise to the level of intuition, until those who were unacquainted with his methods would look askance at him as on a man whose knowledge was not that of other mortals. When I saw him that afternoon so enwrapped in the music at St. James's Hall, I felt that an evil time might be coming upon those whom he had set himself to hunt down.

18

'You want to go home, no doubt, doctor,' he remarked, as we emerged.

'Yes, it would be as well.'

'And I have some business to do which will take some hours. This business at Saxe-Coburg Square is serious.'

'Why serious?'

'A considerable crime is in contemplation. I have every reason to believe that we shall be in time to stop it. But today being Saturday rather complicates matters. I shall want your help tonight.'

'At what time?'

'Ten will be early enough.'

'I shall be at Baker Street at ten.'

'Very well. And, I say, doctor! there may be some little danger, so kindly put your army revolver in your pocket.' He waved his hand, turned on his heel, and disappeared in an instant among the crowd.

I trust that I am not more dense than my neighbours, but I was always oppressed with a sense of my own stupidity in my dealings with Sherlock Holmes. Here I had heard what he had heard, I had seen what he had seen, and yet from his words it was evident that he saw clearly not only what had happened, but what was about to happen, while to me the whole business was still confused and grotesque. As I drove home to my house in Kensington I thought over it all, from the extraordinary story of the red-headed copier of the Encyclopaedia down to the visit to Saxe-Coburg Square, and the ominous words with which he had parted from me. What was this nocturnal expedition, and why should I go armed? Where were we going, and what were we to do? I had the hint from Holmes that this smooth-faced pawnbroker's assistant was a formidable man—a man who might play a deep game. I tried to puzzle it out, but gave it up in despair, and set the matter aside until night should bring an explanation.

19

It was a quarter-past nine when I started from home and made my way across the Park, and so through Oxford Street to Baker Street. Two hansoms were standing at the door, and, as I entered the passage, I heard the sound of voices from above. On entering his room, I found Holmes in animated conversation with two men, one of whom I recognized as Peter Jones, the official police agent; while the other was a long, thin, sad-faced man, with a very shiny hat and oppressively respectable frock coat.

'Ha! our party is complete,' said Holmes, buttoning up his pea-jacket, and taking his heavy hunting crop from the rack. 'Watson, I think you know Mr Jones, of Scotland Yard? Let me introduce you to Mr Merryweather, who is to be our companion in tonight's adventure.'

'We're hunting in couples again, doctor, you see,' said Jones, in his consequential way. 'Our friend here is a wonderful man for starting a chase. All he wants is an old dog to help him do the running down.'

'I hope a wild goose may not prove to be the end of our chase,' observed Mr Merryweather gloomily.

'You may place considerable confidence in Mr Holmes, sir,' said the police agent loftily. 'He has his own little methods, which are, if he won't mind my saying so, just a little too theoretical and fantastic, but he has the makings of a detective in him. It is not too much to say that once or twice, as in that business of the Sholto murder and the Agra treasure, he has been more nearly correct than the official force.'

'Oh, if you say so, Mr Jones, it is all right!' said the stranger, with deference. 'Still, I confess that I miss my rubber. It is the first Saturday night for seven-and-twenty years that I have not had my rubber.'

'I think you will find,' said Sherlock Holmes, 'that you will play for a higher stake tonight than you have ever done yet, and that the play will be more exciting. For you, Mr Merryweather, the stake will be some thirty thousand pounds; and for you, Jones, it will be the man upon whom you wish to lay your hands.'

20

'John Clay, the murderer, thief, smasher, and forger. He's a young man, Mr Merryweather, but he is at the head of his profession, and I would rather have my bracelets on him than on any criminal in London. He's a remarkable man, this young John Clay. His grandfather was a Royal Duke, and he himself has been to Eton and Oxford. His brain is as cunning as his fingers, and though we meet signs of him at every turn, we never know where to find the man himself. He'll crack a crib in Scotland one week, and be raising money to build an orphanage in Cornwall the next. I've been on his track for years, and have never set eyes on him yet.'

'I hope that I may have the pleasure of introducing you tonight. I've had one or two little turns also with Mr John Clay, and I agree with you that he is at the head of his profession. It is past ten, however, and quite time that we started. If you two will take the first hansom, Watson and I will follow in the second.'

Sherlock Holmes was not very communicative during the long drive, and lay back in the cab humming the tunes which he had heard in the afternoon. We rattled through an endless labyrinth of gaslit streets until we emerged into Farringdon Street.

'We are close there now,' my friend remarked. 'This fellow Merryweather is a bank director and personally interested in the matter. I thought it as well to have Jones with us also. He is not a bad fellow, though an absolute imbecile in his profession. He has one positive virtue. He is as brave as a bulldog, and as tenacious as a lobster if he gets his claws upon anyone. Here we are, and they are waiting for us.'

We had reached the same crowded thoroughfare in which we had found ourselves in the morning. Our cabs were dismissed, and following the guidance of Mr Merryweather, we passed down a narrow passage, and through a side door which he opened for us. Within there was a small corridor, which ended in a very massive iron gate. This also was opened, and led down a flight of winding stone steps, which terminated at another formidable gate. Mr Merryweather stopped to light a lantern, and then conducted us down a dark, earth-smelling passage, and so, after opening a third door, into a huge vault or cellar, which was piled all round with crates and massive boxes.

21

'You are not very vulnerable from above,' Holmes remarked, as he held up the lantern and gazed about him.

'Nor from below,' said Mr Merryweather, striking his stick upon the flags which lined the floor. 'Why, dear me, it sounds quite hollow!' he remarked, looking up in surprise.

'I must really ask you to be a little more quiet,' said Holmes severely. 'You have already imperilled the whole success of our expedition. Might I beg that you would have the goodness to sit down upon one of those boxes, and not to interfere?'

The solemn Mr Merryweather perched himself upon a crate, with a very injured expression upon his face, while Holmes fell upon his knees upon the floor, and, with the lantern and a magnifying lens, began to examine minutely the cracks between the stones. A few seconds sufficed to satisfy him, for he sprang to his feet again, and put his glass in his pocket.

'We have at least an hour before us,' he remarked, 'for they can hardly take any steps until the good pawnbroker is safely in bed. Then they will not lose a minute, for the sooner they do their work the longer time they will have for their escape. We are at present, doctor—as no doubt you have divined—in the cellar of the City branch of one of the principal London banks. Mr Merryweather is the chairman of directors, and he will explain to you that there are reasons why the more daring criminals of London should take a considerable interest in this cellar at present.'

'It is our French gold,' whispered the director. 'We have had several warnings that an attempt might be made upon it.'

'Your French gold?'

'Yes. We had occasion some months ago to strengthen our

resources, and borrowed, for that purpose, thirty thousand napoleons from the Bank of France. It has become known that we have never had occasion to unpack the money, and that it is still lying in our cellar. The crate upon which I sit contains two thousand napoleons packed between layers of lead foil. Our reserve of bullion is much larger at present than is usually kept in a single branch office, and the directors have had misgivings upon the subject.'

22

'Which were very well justified,' observed Holmes. 'And now it is time that we arranged our little plans. I expect that within an hour matters will come to a head. In the meantime, Mr Merryweather, we must put the screen over that dark lantern.'

'And sit in the dark?'

'I am afraid so. I had brought a pack of cards in my pocket, and I thought that, as we were a *partie carree*, you might have your rubber after all. But I see that the enemy's preparations have gone so far that we cannot risk the presence of a light. And, first of all, we must choose our positions. These are daring men, and, though we shall take them at a disadvantage, they may do us some harm, unless we are careful. I shall stand behind this crate, and do you conceal yourself behind those. Then, when I flash a light upon them, close in swiftly. If they fire, Watson, have no compunction about shooting them down.'

I placed my revolver, cocked, upon the top of the wooden case behind which I crouched. Holmes shot the slide across the front of his lantern, and left us in pitch darkness—such an absolute darkness as I have never before experienced. The smell of hot metal remained to assure us that the light was still there, ready to flash out at a moment's notice. To me, with my nerves worked up to a pitch of expectancy, there was something depressing and subduing in the sudden gloom, and in the cold, dank air of the vault.

'They have but one retreat,' whispered Holmes. 'That is back through the house into Saxe-Coburg Square. I hope that you have done what I asked you, Jones?'

'I have an inspector and two officers waiting at the front door.'

'Then we have stopped all the holes. And now we must be silent and wait.'

23

What a time it seemed! From comparing notes afterwards, it was but an hour and a quarter, yet it appeared to me that the night must have almost gone, and the dawn be breaking above us. My limbs were weary and stiff, for I feared to change my position, yet my nerves were worked up to the highest pitch of tension, and my hearing was so acute that I could not only hear the gentle breathing of my companions, but I could distinguish the deeper, heavier inbreath of the bulky Jones from the thin, sighing note of the bank director. From my position I could look over the case in the direction of the floor. Suddenly my eyes caught the glint of a light.

At first it was but a lurid spark upon the stone pavement. Then it lengthened out until it became a yellow line, and then, without any warning or sound, a gash seemed to open and a hand appeared, a white, almost womanly hand, which felt about in the centre of the little area of light. For a minute or more the hand, with its writhing fingers, protruded out of the floor. Then it was withdrawn as suddenly as it appeared, and all was dark again save the single lurid spark, which marked a chink between the stones.

Its disappearance, however, was but momentary. With a rending, tearing sound, one of the broad white stones turned over upon its side, and left a square, gaping hole, through which streamed the light of a lantern. Over the edge there peeped a clean-cut, boyish face, which looked keenly about it, and then, with a hand on either side of the aperture, drew itself shoulder-high and waist-high, until one knee rested upon the edge. In another instant he stood at the side of the hole, and was hauling after him a companion, lithe and small like himself, with a pale face and a shock of very red hair.

'It's all clear,' he whispered. 'Have you the chisel and the bags? Great Scott! Jump, Archie, jump, and I'll swing for it!'

24

Sherlock Holmes had sprung out and seized the intruder by the collar. The other dived down the hole, and I heard the sound of rending cloth as Jones clutched at his skirts. The light flashed upon the barrel of a revolver, but Holmes's hunting crop came down on the man's wrist, and the pistol clinked upon the stone floor.

'It's no use, John Clay,' said Holmes blandly, 'you have no chance at all.'

'So I see,' the other answered, with the utmost coolness. 'I fancy that my pal is all right, though I see you have got his coat-tails.'

'There are three men waiting for him at the door,' said Holmes.

'Oh, indeed. You seem to have done the thing very completely. I must compliment you.'

'And I you,' Holmes answered. 'Your red-headed idea was

very new and effective.'

'You'll see your pal again presently,' said Jones. 'He's quicker at climbing down holes than I am. Just hold out while I fix the derbies.'

'I beg that you will not touch me with your filthy hands,' remarked our prisoner, as the handcuffs clattered upon his wrists. 'You may not be aware that I have royal blood in my veins. Have the goodness also, when you address me, always to say "sir" and "please".'

'All right,' said Jones, with a stare and a snigger. 'Well, would you please, sir, march upstairs where we can get a cab to carry your highness to the police station?'

'That is better,' said John Clay serenely. He made a sweeping bow to the three of us, and walked quietly off in the custody of the detective.

'Really, Mr Holmes,' said Mr Merryweather, as we followed them from the cellar, 'I do not know how the bank can thank you or repay you. There is no doubt that you have detected and defeated in the most complete manner one of the most determined attempts at bank robbery that have ever come within my experience.'

25

'I have had one or two little scores of my own to settle with Mr John Clay,' said Holmes. 'I have been at some small expense over this matter, which I shall expect the bank to refund, but beyond that I am amply repaid by having had an experience which is in many ways unique, and by hearing the very remarkable narrative of the Red-headed League.'

'You see, Watson,' he explained, in the early hours of the morning, as we sat over a glass of whisky and soda in Baker

Street, 'it was perfectly obvious from the first that the only possible object of this rather fantastic business of the advertisement of the League, and the copying of the Encyclopaedia must be to get this not over-bright pawnbroker out of the way for a number of hours every day. It was a curious way of managing it, but really it would be difficult to suggest a better. The method was no doubt suggested to Clay's ingenious mind by the colour of his accomplice's hair. The four pounds a week was a lure which must draw him, and what was it to them, who were playing for thousands? They put in the advertisement, one rogue has the temporary office, the other rogue incites the man to apply for it, and together they manage to secure his absence every morning in the week. From the time that I heard of the assistant having come for half wages, it was obvious to me that he had some strong motive for securing the situation.'

'But how could you guess what the motive was?'

'Had there been women in the house, I should have suspected a mere vulgar intrigue. That, however, was out of the question. The man's business was a small one, and there was nothing in his house which could account for such elaborate preparations, and such an expenditure as they were at. It must then be something out of the house. What could it be? I thought of the assistant's fondness for photography, and his trick of vanishing into the cellar. The cellar! There was the end of this tangled clew. Then I made inquiries as to this mysterious assistant, and found that I had to deal with one of the coolest and most daring criminals in London. He was doing something in the cellar—something which took many hours a day for months on end. What could it be, once more? I could think of nothing save that he was running a tunnel to some other building.'

26

'So far I had got when we went to visit the scene of action. I surprised you by beating upon the pavement with my stick. I was ascertaining whether the cellar stretched out in front or behind. It was not in front. Then I rang the bell, and, as I hoped, the assistant answered it. We have had some skirmishes, but we had never set eyes upon each other before. I hardly looked at his face. His knees were what I wished to see. You must yourself have remarked how worn, wrinkled, and stained they were. They spoke of those hours of burrowing. The only remaining point was what they were burrowing for. I walked round the corner, saw that the City and Suburban Bank abutted on our friend's premises, and felt that I had solved my problem. When you drove home after the concert I called upon Scotland Yard, and upon the chairman of the bank directors, with the result that you have seen.'

'And how could you tell that they would make their attempt tonight?' I asked.

'Well, when they closed their League offices that was a sign that they cared no longer about Mr Jabez Wilson's presence; in other words, that they had completed their tunnel. But it was essential that they should use it soon, as it might be discovered, or the bullion might be removed. Saturday would suit them better than any other day, as it would give them two days for their escape. For all these reasons I expected them to come tonight.'

'You reasoned it out beautifully,' I exclaimed, in unfeigned admiration. 'It is so long a chain, and yet every link rings true.'

'It saved me from ennui,' he answered, yawning. 'Alas! I already feel it closing in upon me. My life is spent in one long effort to escape from the commonplaces of existence. These little problems help me to do so.'

'And you are a benefactor of the race,' said I. He shrugged his shoulders. 'Well, perhaps, after all, it is of some little use,' he remarked. '"L'homme c'est rien—l'oeuvre c'est tout," as Gustave Flaubert wrote to Georges Sands.'

THE LODGER

Marie Belloc Lowndes

'There he is at last, and I'm glad of it, Ellen. 'Tain't a night you would wish a dog to be out in.'

Mr Bunting's voice was full of unmistakable relief. He was close to the fire, sitting back in a deep leather armchair—a clean-shaven, dapper man, still in outward appearance what he had been so long, and now no longer was—a self-respecting butler.

'You needn't feel so nervous about him; Mr Sleuth can look out for himself, all right.' Mrs Bunting spoke in a dry, rather tart tone. She was less emotional, better balanced, than was her husband. On her the marks of past servitude were less apparent, but they were there all the same—especially in her neat black stuff dress and scrupulously clean, plain collar and cuffs. Mrs Bunting, as a single woman, had been for long years what is known as a useful maid.

'I can't think why he wants to go out in such weather. He did it in last week's fog, too,' Bunting went on complaining.

'Well, it's none of your business—now, is it?'

'No; that's true enough. Still, 'twould be a very bad thing for us if anything happened to him. This lodger's the first bit of luck we've had for a very long time.'

Mrs Bunting made no answer to this remark. It was too obviously true to be worth answering. Also she was listening—following in imagination her lodger's quick, singularly quiet—stealthy, she called it to herself—progress through the dark, fog-filled hall and up the staircase.

'It isn't safe for decent folk to be out in such weather—not unless they have something to do that won't wait till tomorrow.' Bunting had at last turned round. He was now looking straight into his wife's narrow, colourless face; he was an obstinate man, and liked to prove himself right. 'I read you out the accidents in *Lloyd's* yesterday—shocking, they were, and all brought about by the fog! And then, that 'orrid monster at his work again—'

'Monster?' repeated Mrs Bunting absently. She was trying to hear the lodger's footsteps overhead; but her husband went on as if there had been no interruption:

'It wouldn't be very pleasant to run up against such a party as that in the fog, eh?'

'What stuff you do talk!' she said sharply; and then she got up suddenly. Her husband's remark had disturbed her. She hated to think of such things as the terrible series of murders that were just then horrifying and exciting the nether world of London. Though she enjoyed pathos and sentiment—Mrs Bunting would listen with mild amusement to the details of a breach-of-promise action—she shrank from stories of either immorality or physical violence.

Mrs Bunting got up from the straight-backed chair on which she had been sitting. It would soon be time for supper.

She moved about the sitting-room, flecking off an imperceptible touch of dust here, straightening a piece of furniture there.

Bunting looked around once or twice. He would have liked

to ask Ellen to leave off fidgeting, but he was mild and fond of peace, so he refrained. However, she soon gave over what irritated him of her own accord.

But even then Mrs Bunting did not at once go down to the cold kitchen, where everything was in readiness for her simple cooking. Instead, she opened the door leading into the bedroom behind, and there, closing the door quietly, stepped back into the darkness and stood motionless, listening.

At first she heard nothing, but gradually there came the sound of someone moving about in the room just overhead; try as she might, however, it was impossible for her to guess what her lodger was doing. At last she heard him open the door leading out on the landing. That meant that he would spend the rest of the evening in the rather cheerless room above the drawing-room floor—oddly enough, he liked sitting there best, though the only warmth obtainable was from a gas-stove fed by a shilling-in-the slot arrangement.

It was indeed true that Mr Sleuth had brought the Buntings luck, for at the time he had taken their rooms it had been touch-and-go with them.

After having each separately led the sheltered, impersonal, and, above all, the financially easy existence that is the compensation life offers to those men and women who deliberately take upon themselves the yoke of domestic service, these two, butler and useful maid, had suddenly, in middle age, determined to join their fortunes and savings.

Bunting was a widower; he had one pretty daughter, a girl of seventeen, who now lived, as had been the case ever since the death of her mother, with a prosperous aunt. His second wife had been reared in the Foundling Hospital, but she had gradually worked her way up into the higher ranks of the servant class and as useful maid she had saved quite a tidy sum of money.

Unluckily, misfortune had dogged Mr and Mrs Bunting from the very first. The seaside place where they had begun by taking a lodging-house became the scene of an epidemic. Then had followed a business experiment which had proved disastrous. But before going back into service, either together or separately, they had made up their minds to make one last effort, and, with the little money that remained to them, they had taken over the lease of a small house in the Marylebone Road.

Bunting, whose appearance was very good, had retained a connection with old employers and their friends, so he occasionally got a good job as waiter. During this last month his jobs had perceptibly increased in number and in profit; Mrs Bunting was not superstitious, but it seemed that in this matter, as in everything else, Mr Sleuth, their new lodger, had brought them luck.

As she stood there, still listening intently in the darkness of the bedroom, she told herself, not for the first time, what Mr Sleuth's departure would mean to her and Bunting. It would almost certainly mean ruin.

Luckily, the lodger seemed entirely pleased both with the rooms and with his landlady. There was really no reason why he should ever leave such nice lodgings. Mrs Bunting shook off her vague sense of apprehension and unease. She turned round, took a step forward, and, feeling for the handle of the door giving into the passage, she opened it, and went down with light, firm steps into the kitchen.

She lit the gas and put a frying-pan on the stove, and then once more her mind reverted, as if in spite of herself, to her lodger, and there came back to Mrs Bunting, very vividly, the memory of all that had happened the day Mr Sleuth had taken her rooms.

The date of this excellent lodger's coming had been the twenty-ninth of December, and the time late afternoon. She and Bunting had been sitting, gloomily enough over their small banked-up fire. They had dined in the middle of the day—he on a couple of sausages, she on a little cold ham. They were utterly out of heart, each trying to pluck up courage to tell the other that it was no use trying any more. The two had also had a little tiff on that dreary afternoon. A newspaper-seller had come yelling down the Marylebone Road, shouting out, 'Orrible murder in Whitechapel!' and just because Bunting had an old uncle living in the East End he had gone and bought a paper, and at a time, too, when every penny, nay, every half-penny, had its full value! Mrs Bunting remembered the circumstances because that murder in Whitechapel had been the first of these terrible cringes—there had been four since—which she would never allow Bunting to discuss in her presence, and yet which had of late begun to interest curiously, uncomfortably, ever her refined mind.

But, to return to the lodger. It was then, on that dreary afternoon, that suddenly there had come to the front door a tremulous, uncertain double knock.

Bunting ought to have got up, but he had gone on reading the paper and so Mrs Bunting, with the woman's greater courage, had gone out into the passage, turned up the gas, and opened the door to see who it could be. She remembered, as if it were yesterday instead of nigh on a month ago, Mr Sleuth's peculiar appearance. Tall, dark, lanky, an old-fashioned top hat concealing his high bald forehead, he had stood there, an odd figure of a man, blinking at her.

'I believe—is it not a fact that you let lodgings?' he had asked in a hesitating, whistling voice, a voice that she had known in a moment to be that of an educated man—of a gentleman. As he had stepped into the hall, she had noticed that in his right hand he held a narrow bag—a quite new bag of strong brown leather.

Everything had been settled in less than a quarter of an hour. Mr Sleuth had at once 'taken' to the drawing-room floor, and then, as Mrs Bunting eagerly lit the gas in the front room above, he had looked around him and said, rubbing his hands with a nervous movement, 'Capital—capital! This is just what I've been looking for!'

The sink had specially pleased him—the sink and the gas-stove. 'This is quite first-rate!' he had exclaimed, 'for I make all sorts of experiments. I am, you must understand, Mrs—er—Bunting, a man of science.' Then he had sat down—suddenly. 'I'm very tired,' he had said in a low tone, 'very tired indeed! I have been walking about all day.'

From the very first the lodger's manner had been odd, sometimes distant and abrupt, and then, for no reason at all that she could see, confidential and plaintively confiding. But Mrs Bunting was aware that eccentricity has always been a perquisite, as it were the special luxury, of the well born and well educated. Scholars and such-like are never quite like other people.

And then, this particular gentleman had proved himself so eminently satisfactory as to the one thing that really matters to those who let lodgings. 'My name is Sleuth,' he said, 'S-l-e-u-t-h. Think of a hound, Mrs Bunting, and you'll never forget my name. I could give you references,' he had added, giving her, as she now remembered, a funny sidewise look, 'but I prefer to dispense with them. How much did you say? Twenty-three shillings a week, with attendance? Yes, that will suit me perfectly; and I'll begin by paying my first month's rent in advance. Now, four times twenty-three shillings is'—he looked at Mrs Bunting, and for the first time he smiled, a queer, wry smile—'ninety-two shillings.'

He had taken a handful of sovereigns out of his pocket and put them down on the table. 'Look here,' he had said, 'there's five pounds; and you can keep the change, for I shall want you to do a little shopping for me tomorrow'

After he had been in the house about an hour, the bell had rung, and the new lodger had asked Mrs Bunting if she could oblige him with the loan of a Bible. She brought up to him her best Bible, the one that had been given to her as a wedding present by a lady with whose mother she had lived for several years. This Bible and one other book, of which the odd name was *Cruden's Concordance*, formed Mr Sleuth's only reading: he spent hours each day poring over the Old Testament and over the volume which Mrs Bunting had at last decided to give to be a queer kind of index to the Book.

However, to return to the lodger's first arrival. He had had no luggage with him, barring the small brown bag, but very soon parcels had begun to arrive addressed to Mr Sleuth, and it was then that Mrs Bunting first became curious. These parcels were full of clothes; but it was quite clear to the landlady's feminine eye that none of these clothes had been made for Mr Sleuth. They were, in fact, second-hand clothes, bought at good second-hand places, each marked, when marked at all, with a different name. And the really extraordinary thing was that occasionally a complete suit disappeared—became, as it were, obliterated from the lodger's wardrobe.

As for the bag he had brought with him, Mrs Bunting had never caught sight of it again. And this also was certainly very strange.

Mrs Bunting thought a great deal about that bag. She often wondered what had been in it; not a nightshirt and comb and brush, as she had at first supposed, for Mr Sleuth had asked her to go out and buy him a brush and comb and toothbrush the morning after his arrival. That fact was specially impressed on her memory, for at the little shop, a barber's, where she had purchased the brush and comb, the foreigner who had served her had insisted on telling her some of the horrible details of the murder that had taken place the day before in Whitechapel, and it had upset her very much.

As to where the bag was now, it was probably locked up in the lower part of a chiffonnier in the front sitting-room. Mr Sleuth evidently always carried the key of the little cupboard on his person, for Mrs Bunting, though she looked well for it, had never been able to find it.

And yet, never was there a more confiding or trusting gentleman. The first four days that he had been with them he had allowed his money—the considerable sum of one hundred and eighty-four pounds in gold—to lie about wrapped up in pieces of paper on his dressing-table. This was a very foolish, indeed a wrong thing to do, as she had allowed herself respectfully to point out to him; but as an only answer he had laughed, a loud, discordant shout of laughter.

Mr Sleuth had many other odd ways; but Mrs Bunting, a true woman in spite of her prim manner and love of order, had an infinite patience with masculine vagaries.

On the first morning of Mr Sleuth's stay in the Buntings's house, while Mrs Bunting was out buying things for him, the new lodger had turned most of the pictures and photographs hanging in his sitting-room with their faces to the wall! But this queer action on Mr Sleuth's part had not surprised

Mrs Bunting as much as it might have done; it recalled an incident of her long-past youth—something that had happened a matter of twenty years ago, at a time when Mrs Bunting, then the still youthful Ellen Cottrell, had been maid to an old lady. The old lady had a favourite nephew, a bright, jolly young gentleman who had been learning to paint animals in Paris; and it was he who had had the impudence, early one summer morning, to turn to the wall six beautiful engravings of paintings done by the famous Mr Landseer! The old lady thought the world of those pictures, but her nephew, as the only excuse for the extraordinary thing he had done, had observed that 'they put his eye out'.

Mr Sleuth's excuse had been much the same; for, when Mrs Bunting had come into his sitting-room and found all her pictures, or at any rate all those of her pictures that happened to be portraits of ladies, with their faces to the wall, he had offered an only explanation, 'Those women's eyes follow me about.' Mrs Bunting had gradually become aware that Mr Sleuth had a fear and dislike of women. When she was 'doing' the staircase and landing, she often heard him reading bits of the Bible aloud to himself, and in the majority of instances the texts he chose contained uncomplimentary reference to her own sex. Only today she had stopped and listened while he uttered threateningly the awful words, 'A strange woman is a narrow pit. She also lieth in wait as for a prey, and increaseth the transgressors among men.' There had been a pause, and then had come, in a high singsong, 'Her house is the way to hell, going down to the chambers of death.' It had made Mrs Bunting feel quite queer.

The lodger's daily habits were also peculiar. He stayed in bed all morning, and sometimes part of the afternoon, and he never went out before the street lamps were alight. Then, there was his dislike of an open fire; he generally sat in the top front room, and while there he always used the large gas-stove, not only for his experiments, which he carried on at night, but also in the daytime, for warmth.

But there! Where was the use of worrying about the lodger's funny ways? Of course, Mr Sleuth was eccentric; if he hadn't been 'just a leetle "touched" upstairs'—as Bunting had once described it—he wouldn't be their lodger now; he would be living in a quite different sort of way with some of his relations, or with a friend of his own class.

Mrs Bunting, while these thoughts galloped disconnectedly through her brain, went on with her cooking, doing everything with a certain delicate and clean precision.

While in the middle of making the toast on which was to be poured some melted cheese, she suddenly heard a noise, or rather a series of noises. Shuffling, hesitating steps were creaking down the house above. She looked up and listened. Surely Mr Sleuth was not going out again into the cold, foggy night? But no; for the sounds did not continue down the passage leading to the front door.

The heavy steps were coming slowly down the kitchen stairs. Nearer and nearer came the thudding sounds, and Mrs Bunting's heart began to beat as if in response. She put out the gas-stove, unheedful of the fact that the cheese would stiffen and spoil in the cold air; and then she turned and faced the door. There was a fumbling at the handle, and a moment later the door opened and revealed, as she had known it would, her lodger.

Mr Sleuth was clad in a plaid dressing-gown, and in his hand was a candle. When he saw the lit-up kitchen, and the woman standing in it, he looked inexplicably taken aback, almost aghast.

'Yes, sir? What can I do for you, sir? I hope you didn't ring, sir?' Mrs Bunting did not come forward to meet her lodger; instead, she held her ground in front of the stove. Mr Sleuth had no business to come down like this into her kitchen.

'No, I—I didn't ring,' he stammered; 'I didn't know you were down here, Mrs Bunting. Please excuse my costume. The truth is, my gas-stove has gone wrong, or, rather, that shilling in-the-slot arrangement has done so. I came down to see if *you* had a gas-stove. I am going to ask leave to use it tonight for an experiment I want to make.'

Mrs Bunting felt troubled—oddly, unnaturally troubled. Why couldn't the lodger's experiment wait till tomorrow? 'Oh, certainly, sir; but you will find it very cold down here.' She looked round her dubiously.

'It seems most pleasantly warm,' he observed, 'warm and cosy after my cold room upstairs.'

'Won't you let me make you a fire?' Mrs Bunting's housewifely instincts were roused. 'Do let me make you a fire in your bedroom, sir; I'm sure you ought to have one there these cold nights.'

'By no means—I mean, I would prefer not. I do not like an open fire, Mrs Bunting.' He frowned, and still stood, a strange-looking figure, just inside the kitchen door.

'Do you want to use this stove now, sir? Is there anything I can do to help you?'

'No, not now—thank you all the same, Mrs Bunting. I shall come down later, altogether later—probably after you and your husband have gone to bed. But I should be much obliged if you would see that the gas people come tomorrow and put my stove in order.'

'Perhaps Bunting could put it right for you, sir. I'll ask him to go up.'

'No, no—I don't want anything of that sort done tonight. Besides, he couldn't put it right. The cause of the trouble is quite simple. The machine is choked up with shillings: a foolish plan, so I have always felt it to be.'

Mr Sleuth spoke very pettishly, with far more heat than he was wont to speak; but Mrs Bunting sympathized with him. She had always suspected those slot-machines to be as dishonest as if they were human. It was dreadful, the way they swallowed up the shillings!

As if he were divining her thoughts, Mr Sleuth, walking forward, stared up at the kitchen slot-machine. 'Is it nearly full?' he asked abruptly. 'I expect my experiment will take some time, Mrs Bunting.'

'Oh, no, sir; there's plenty of room for shillings there still. We don't use our stove as much as you do yours, sir. I'm never in the kitchen a minute longer than I can help in this cold weather.'

And then, with him preceding her, Mrs Bunting and her lodger made a slow progress to the ground floor. There Mr Sleuth courteously bade his landlady goodnight, and proceeded upstairs to his own apartment.

Mrs Bunting again went down into her kitchen, again she lit the stove, and again she cooked the toasted cheese. But she felt unnerved, afraid of she knew not what. The place seemed to her alive with alien presences, and once she caught herself listening, which was absurd, for of course she could not hope to hear what her lodger was doing two, if not three, flights upstairs. She had never been able to discover what Mr Sleuth's experiments really were; all she knew was that they required a very high degree of heat.

The Buntings went to bed early that night. But Mrs Bunting

intended to stay awake. She wanted to know at what hour of the night her lodger would come down into the kitchen, and, above all, she was anxious as to how long he would stay there. But she had had a long day, and presently she fell asleep.

The church clock hard by struck two in the morning, and suddenly Mrs Bunting awoke. She felt sharply annoyed with herself. How could she have dropped off like that? Mr Sleuth must have been down and up again hours ago.

Then, gradually, she became aware of a faint acrid odour; elusive, almost intangible, it yet seemed to encompass her and the snoring man by her side almost as a vapour might have done.

Mrs Bunting sat up in bed and sniffed; and then, in spite of the cold, she quietly crept out of the nice, warm bedclothes and crawled along to the bottom of the bed. There Mr Sleuth's landlady did a very curious thing; she leaned over the brass rail and put her face close to the hinge of the door. Yes, it was from there that this strange, horrible odour was coming; the smell must be very strong in the passage. Mrs Bunting thought she knew now what became of those suits of clothes of Mr Sleuth's that disappeared.

As she crept back, shivering, under the bedclothes, she longed to give her sleeping husband a good shake, and in fancy she heard herself saying: 'Bunting, get up! There is something strange going on downstairs that we ought to know about.'

But Mr Sleuth's landlady, as she lay by her husband's side, listening with painful intentness, knew very well that she would do nothing of the sort. The lodger had a right to destroy his clothes by burning if the fancy took him. What if he did make a certain amount of mess, a certain amount of smell, in her nice kitchen? Was he not—was he not such a good lodger! If they did anything to upset him, where could they ever hope to get another like him?

Three o'clock struck before Mrs Bunting heard slow, heavy steps creaking up her kitchen stairs. But Mr Sleuth did not go straight up to his own quarters, as she expected him to do. Instead, he went to the front door, and, opening it, put it on the chain. At the end of ten minutes or so he closed the front door, and by that time Mrs Bunting had divined why the lodger had behaved in this strange fashion—it must have been to get the strong acrid smell of burning wool out of the passage. But Mrs Bunting felt as if she herself would never get rid of the horrible odour. She felt herself to be all smell.

At last the unhappy woman fell into a deep, troubled sleep; and then she dreamed a most terrible and unnatural dream; hoarse voices seemed to be shouting in her ear, ''Orrible murder off the Edgeware Road!' Then three words, indistinctly uttered, followed by '—at his work again! Awful details!'

Even in her dream Mrs Bunting felt angered and impatient; she knew so well why she was being disturbed by this horrid nightmare. It was because of Bunting—Bunting, who insisted on talking to her of those frightful murders, in which only morbid, vulgar-minded people took any interest. Why, even now, in her dream, she could hear her husband speaking to her about it.

'Ellen'—so she heard Bunting say in her ear—'Ellen, my dear, I am just going to get up to get a paper. It's after seven o'clock.'

Mrs Bunting sat up in bed. The shouting, nay, worse, the sound of tramping, hurrying feet smote on her ears. It had been no nightmare, then, but something infinitely worse—reality. Why couldn't Bunting have lain quietly in bed awhile longer, and let his poor wife go on dreaming? The most awful dream would have been easier to bear than this awakening.

She heard her husband go to the front door, and, as he bought the paper, exchange a few excited words with the newspaper boy. Then he came back and began silently moving about the room.

'Well!' she cried. 'Why don't you tell me about it?'

'I thought you'd rather not hear.'

'Of course I like to know what happens close to our own front door!' she snapped out.

And then he read out a piece of the newspaper—only a few lines, after all—telling in brief, unemotional language that the body of a woman, apparently done to death in a peculiarly atrocious fashion some hours before, had been found in a passage leading to a disused warehouse off the Marylebone Road.

'It serves that sort of hussy right!' was Mrs Bunting's only comment.

When Mrs Bunting went down into the kitchen, everything there looked just as she had left it, and there was no trace of the acrid smell she had expected to find there. Instead, the cavernous whitewashed room was full of fog, and she noticed that, though the shutters were bolted and barred as she had left them, the windows behind them had been widely opened to the air. She, of course, had left them shut.

She stooped and flung open the oven door of her gas-stove. Yes, it was as she had expected; a fierce heat had been generated there since she had last used the oven, and a mass of black, gluey soot had fallen through to the stone floor below.

Mrs Bunting took the ham and eggs that she had bought the previous day for her own and Bunting's breakfast, and broiled them over the gas-ring in their sitting-room. Her husband watched her in surprised silence. She had never done such a thing before.

'I couldn't stay down there,' she said, 'it was so cold and foggy. I thought I'd make breakfast up here, just for today.'

'Yes,' he said kindly; 'that's quite right, Ellen. I think you've done quite right, my dear.'

But, when it came to the point, his wife could not eat any of the nice breakfast she had got ready; she only had another cup of tea.

'Are you ill?' Bunting asked solicitously.

'No,' she said shortly; 'of course I'm not ill. Don't be silly! The thought of that horrible thing happening so close by has upset me. Just hark to them, now!'

Through their closed windows penetrated the sound of scurrying feet and loud, ribald laughter. A crowd, nay, a mob, hastened to and from the scene of the murder.

Mrs Bunting made her husband lock the front gate. 'I don't want any of those ghouls in here!' she exclaimed angrily. And then, 'What a lot of idle people there must be in the world,' she said.

The coming and going went on all day. Mrs Bunting stayed indoors; Bunting went out. After all, the ex-butler was human— it was natural that he should feel thrilled and excited. All their neighbours were the same. His wife wasn't reasonable about such things. She quarrelled with him when he didn't tell her anything, and yet he was sure she would have been angry with him if he had said very much about it.

The lodger's bell rang about two o'clock, and Mrs Bunting prepared the simple luncheon that was also his breakfast. As she rested the tray a minute on the drawing-room floor landing, she heard Mr Sleuth's high, quavering voice reading aloud the words:

'She saith to him, Stolen waters are sweet, and bread eaten in secret is pleasant. But he knoweth not that the dead are there; and that her guests are in the depths of hell.'

The landlady turned the handle of the door and walked in with the tray. Mr Sleuth was sitting close by the window, and Mrs Bunting's Bible lay open before him. As she came in he hastily closed the Bible and looked down at the crowd walking along the Marylebone Road.

'There seem a great many people out today,' he observed, without looking round.

'Yes, sir, there do.' Mrs Bunting said nothing more, and offered no other explanation; and the lodger, as he at last turned to his landlady, smiled pleasantly. He had acquired a great liking and respect for this well-behaved, taciturn woman; she was the first person for whom he had felt any such feeling for many years past.

He took a half sovereign out of his waistcoat pocket; Mrs Bunting noticed that it was not the same waistcoat Mr Sleuth had been wearing the day before. 'Will you please accept this half sovereign for the use of your kitchen last night?' he said. 'I made as little mess as I could, but I was carrying on a rather elaborate experiment.'

She held out her hand, hesitated, and then took the coin. As she walked down the stairs, the winter sun, a yellow ball hanging in the smoky sky, glinted in on Mrs Bunting, and lent blood-red gleams, or so it seemed to her, to the piece of gold she was holding in her hand.

It was a very cold night—so cold, so windy, so snow-laden the atmosphere, that every one who could do so stayed indoors. Bunting, however, was on his way home from what had proved a very pleasant job; he had been acting as waiter at a young lady's birthday party, and a remarkable piece of luck had come his way. The young lady had come into a fortune that day, and she had had the gracious, the surprising thought of presenting each of the hired waiters with a sovereign.

This birthday treat had put him in mind of another birthday. His daughter Daisy would be eighteen the following Saturday. Why shouldn't he send her a postal order for half a sovereign, so that she might come up and spend her birthday in London?

Having Daisy for three or four days would cheer up Ellen. Mr Bunting, slackening his footsteps, began to think with puzzled concern of how queer his wife had seemed lately. She had become so nervous, so 'jumpy,' that he didn't know what to make of her sometimes. She had never been a really good-tempered woman, your capable, self-respecting woman seldom is—but she had never been like what she was now. Of late she sometimes got quite hysterical; he had let fall a sharp word to her the other day, and she had sat down on a chair, thrown her black apron over her face, and burst out sobbing violently.

During the last ten days Ellen had taken to talking in her sleep. 'No, no, no!' she had cried out, only the night before. 'It isn't true! I won't have it said! It's a lie!' And there had been a wail of horrible fear and revolt in her unusually quiet, mincing voice. Yes, it would certainly be a good thing for her to have Daisy's company for a bit. Whew! It *was* cold; and Bunting had stupidly forgotten his gloves. He put his hands in his pockets to keep them warm.

Suddenly he became aware that Mr Sleuth, the lodger who seemed to have 'turned their luck', as it were, was walking along on the opposite side of the solitary street.

Mr Sleuth's tall, thin figure was rather bowed, his head bent toward the ground. His right arm was thrust into his long Inverness cape; the other occasionally sawed the air, doubtless in order to help him keep warm. He was walking rather quickly. It was clear that he had not yet become aware of the proximity of his landlord.

Bunting felt pleased to see his lodger; it increased his feeling of general satisfaction. Strange, was it not, that that odd, peculiar-looking figure should have made all the difference to his (Bunting's) and Mrs Bunting's happiness and comfort in life?

Naturally, Bunting saw far less of the lodger than did Mrs Bunting. Their gentleman had made it very clear that he did not like either the husband or wife to come up to his rooms without being definitely asked to do so, and Bunting had been up there only once since Mr Sleuth's arrival five weeks before. This seemed to be a good opportunity for a little genial conversation.

Bunting, still an active man for his years, crossed the road, and, stepping briskly forward, tried to overtake Mr Sleuth; but the more he hurried, the more the other hastened, and that without even turning to see whose steps he heard echoing behind him on the now freezing pavement.

Mr Sleuth's own footsteps were quite inaudible—an odd circumstance, when you came to think of it, as Bunting did think of it later, lying awake by Ellen's side in the pitch-darkness. What it meant was, of course, that the lodger had rubber soles on his shoes.

The two men, the pursued and the pursuer, at last turned into the Marylebone Road. They were now within a hundred yards of home; and so, plucking up courage, Bunting called out, his voice echoing freshly on the still air:

'Mr Sleuth, sir! Mr Sleuth!'

The lodger stopped and turned round. He had been walking so quickly, and he was in so poor a physical condition, that the sweat was pouring down his face.

'Ah! So it's you, Mr Bunting? I heard footsteps behind me, and I hurried on. I wish I'd known that it was only you; there are so many queer characters about at night in London.'

'Not on a night like this, sir. Only honest folk who have business out of doors would be out such a night as this. It is cold, sir!' And then into Bunting's slow and honest mind there suddenly crept the query as to what Mr Sleuth's own business out could be on this cold, bitter night.

'Cold?' the lodger repeated. 'I can't say that I find it cold, Mr Bunting. When the snow falls the air always becomes milder.'

'Yes, sir; but tonight there's such a sharp east wind. Why, it freezes the very marrow in one's bones!'

Bunting noticed that Mr Sleuth kept his distance in a rather strange way: he walked at the edge of the pavement, leaving the rest of it, on the wall side, to his landlord.

'I lost my way,' he said abruptly. 'I've been over Primrose Hill to see a friend of mine, and then, coming back, I lost my way.'

Bunting could well believe that, for when he had first noticed Mr Sleuth he was coming from the east, and not, as he should have done if walking home from Primrose Hill, from the north.

They had now reached the little gate that gave on to the shabby, paved court in front of the house. Mr Sleuth was walking up the flagged path, when, with a 'By your leave, sir,' the ex-butler, stepping aside, slipped in front of his lodger, in order to open the front door for him.

As he passed by Mr Sleuth, the back of Bunting's bare left hand brushed lightly against the long Inverness cape the other man was wearing, and, to his surprise, the stretch of cloth against which his hand lay for a moment was not only damp, damp from the flakes of snow that had settled upon it, but wet—wet and gluey. Bunting thrust his left hand into his pocket; it was with the other that he placed the key in the lock of the door.

The two men passed into the hall together. The house

seemed blackly dark in comparison with the lighted-up road outside; and then, quite suddenly, there came over Bunting a feeling of mortal terror, an instinctive knowledge that some terrible and immediate danger was near him. A voice—the voice of his first wife, the long-dead girl to whom his mind so seldom reverted nowaday suttered in his ear the words, 'Take care!'

'I'm afraid, Mr Bunting, that you must have felt something dirty, foul, on my coat? It's too long a story to tell you now, but I brushed up against a dead animal—a dead rabbit lying across a bench on Primrose Hill.'

Mr Sleuth spoke in a very quiet voice, almost in a whisper.

'No, sir; no, I didn't notice nothing. I scarcely touched you, sir,' It seemed as if a power outside himself compelled Bunting to utter these lying words. 'And now, sir, I'll be saying goodnight to you,' he added.

He waited until the lodger had gone upstairs, and then he turned into his own sitting-room. There he sat down, for he felt very queer. He did not draw his left hand out of his pocket till he heard the other man moving about in the room above. Then he lit the gas and held up his left hand; he put it close to his face. It was flecked, streaked with blood.

He took off his boots, and then, very quietly, he went into the room where his wife lay asleep. Stealthily he walked across to the toilet-table, and dipped his hand into the water-jug.

The next morning Mr Sleuth's landlord awoke with a start; he felt curiously heavy about the limbs and tired about the eyes.

Drawing his watch from under his pillow, he saw that it was nearly nine o'clock. He and Ellen had overslept. Without waking her, he got out of bed and pulled up the blind. It was snowing heavily, and, as is the way when it snows, even in London, it was strangely, curiously still.

After he had dressed he went out into the passage. A newspaper and a letter were lying on the mat. Fancy having slept through the postman's knock! He picked them both up and went into the sitting-room; then he carefully shut the door behind him, and, tossing the letter aside, spread the newspaper wide open on the table and bent over it.

As Bunting at last looked up and straightened himself, a look of inexpressible relief shone upon his stolid face. The item of news he had felt certain would be there, printed in big type on the middle sheet, was not there.

He folded the paper and laid it on a chair, and then eagerly took up his letter.

> Dear Father [it ran]: I hope this finds you as well as it leaves me. Mrs Puddle's youngest child has got scarlet fever, and aunt thinks I had better come away at once, just to stay with you for a few days. Please tell Ellen I won't give her no trouble.
>
> Your loving daughter,
> Daisy

Bunting felt amazingly light-hearted; and, as he walked into the next room, he smiled broadly.

'Ellen,' he cried out, 'here's news! Daisy's coming today. There's scarlet fever in their house, and Martha thinks she had better come away for a few days. She'll be here for her birthday!'

Mrs Bunting listened in silence; she did not even open her eyes. 'I can't have the girl here just now,' she said shortly; 'I've got just as much as I can manage to do.'

But Bunting felt pugnacious, and so cheerful as to be almost light-headed. Deep down in his heart he looked back to last night with a feeling of shame and self-rebuke. Whatever had made such horrible thoughts and suspicions come into his head?

'Of course Daisy will come here,' he said shortly. 'If it comes to that, she'll be able to help you with the work, and she'll brisk us both up a bit.'

Rather to his surprise, Mrs Bunting said nothing in answer to this, and he changed the subject abruptly. 'The lodger and me came in together last night,' he observed. 'He's certainly a funny kind of gentleman. It wasn't the sort of night one would choose to go for a walk over Primrose Hill, and yet that was what he had been doing—so he said.'

It stopped snowing about ten o'clock, and the morning wore itself away.

Just as twelve was striking, a four-wheeler drew up to the gate. It was Daisy—pink-cheeked, excited, laughing-eyed Daisy, a sight to gladden any father's heart. 'Aunt said I was to have a cab if the weather was bad,' she said.

There was a bit of a wrangle over the fare. King's Cross, as all the world knows, is nothing like two miles from the Marylebone Road, but the man clamoured for one-and-sixpence, and hinted darkly that he had done the young lady a favour in bringing her at all.

While he and Bunting were having words, Daisy, leaving them to it, walked up the path to the door where her stepmother was awaiting her.

Suddenly there fell loud shouts on the still air. They sounded strangely eerie, breaking sharply across the muffled, snowy air. 'What's that?' said Bunting, with a look of startled fear. 'Why, whatever's that?'

The cabman lowered his voice: 'Them are crying out that 'orrible affair at King's Cross. He's done for two of 'em this time! That's what I meant when I said I might have got a better fare; I wouldn't say anything before Missy there, but folk 'ave been coming from all over London—like a fire; plenty of toffs, too. But there-there's nothing to see now!'

'What! Another woman murdered last night?' Bunting felt and looked convulsed with horror.

The cabman stared at him, surprised. 'Two of 'em, I tell yer—within a few yards of one another. He 'ave got a nerve—'

'Have they caught him?' asked Bunting perfunctorily.

'Lord, no! They'll never catch 'im! It must 'ave happened hours and hours ago—they was both stone-cold. One each end of an archway. That's why they didn't see 'em before.'

The hoarse cries were coming nearer and nearer—two news vendors trying to outshout each other.

'Orrible discovery near King's Cross!' they yelled exultantly. And as Bunting, with his daughter's bag in his hand, hurried up the path and passed through his front door, the words pursued him like a dreadful threat.

Angrily he shut out the hoarse, insistent cries. No, he had no wish to buy a paper. That kind of crime wasn't fit reading for a young girl, such a girl as was his Daisy, brought up as carefully as if she had been a young lady by her strict Methody aunt.

As he stood in his little hall, trying to feel 'all right' again, he could hear Daisy's voice—high, voluble, excited—giving her stepmother a long account of the scarlet-fever case to which she owed her presence in London. But, as Bunting pushed open the door of the sitting-room there came a note of sharp alarm in his daughter's voice, and he heard her say: 'Why, Ellen! Whatever is the matter? You do look bad!' and his wife's muffled answer: 'Open the window—do.'

Rushing across the room, Bunting pushed up the sash. The

newspaper-sellers were now just outside the house. 'Horrible discovery near King's Cross—a clue to the murderer!' they yelled. And then, helplessly, Mrs Bunting began to laugh. She laughed and laughed and laughed, rocking herself to and fro as if in an ecstasy of mirth.

'Why, father, whatever's the matter with her?' Daisy looked quite scared.

'She's in 'sterics—that's what it is,' he said shortly. 'I'll just get the water-jug. Wait a minute.'

Bunting felt very put out, and yet glad, too, for this queer seizure of Ellen's almost made him forget the sick terror with which he had been possessed a moment before. That he and his wife should be obsessed by the same fear, the same terror, never crossed his simple, slow-working mind.

The lodger's bell rang. That, or the threat of the water-jug, had a magical effect on Mrs Bunting. She rose to her feet, still trembling, but composed.

As Mrs Bunting went upstairs she felt her legs trembling under her, and put out a shaking hand to clutch at the bannister for support. She waited a few minutes on the landing, and then knocked at the door of her lodger's parlour.

But Mr Sleuth's voice answered her from the bedroom. 'I'm not well,' he called out querulously; 'I think I caught a chill going out to see a friend last night. I'd be obliged if you'll bring me up a cup of tea and put it outside my door, Mrs Bunting.'

'Very well, sir.'

Mrs Bunting went downstairs and made her lodger a cup of tea over the gas-ring, Bunting watching her the while in heavy silence.

During their midday dinner the husband and wife had a little discussion as to where Daisy should sleep. It had already been settled that a bed should be made up for her in the sitting-room, but Bunting saw reason to change this plan. As the two women were clearing away the dishes, he looked up and said shortly: 'I think 'twould be better if Daisy were to sleep with you, Ellen and I were to sleep in the sitting-room.'

Ellen acquiesced quietly.

Daisy was a good-natured girl; she liked London, and wanted to make herself useful to her stepmother. 'I'll wash up; don't you bother to come downstairs,' she said.

Bunting began to walk up and down the room. His wife gave him a furtive glance; she wondered what he was thinking about,

'Didn't you get a paper?' she said at last.

'There's the paper,' he said crossly, 'the paper we always do take in, the *Telegraph*.' His look challenged her to a further question.

'I thought they were shouting something in the street—I mean just before I took bad.'

But he made no answer; instead, he went to the top of the staircase and called out sharply: 'Daisy! Daisy, child, are you there?'

'Yes, father,' she answered from below.

'Better come upstairs out of that cold kitchen.'

He came back into the sitting-room again.

'Ellen, is the lodger in? I haven't heard him moving about. I don't want Daisy to be mixed up with him.'

'Mr Sleuth is not well today,' his wife answered; 'he is remaining in bed a bit. Daisy needn't have anything to do with him. She'll have her work cut out looking after things down here. That's where I want her to help me.'

'Agreed,' he said.

When it grew dark, Bunting went out and bought an evening

paper. He read it out of doors in the biting cold, standing beneath a street lamp. He wanted to see what was the clue to the murderer.

The clue proved to be a very slender one—merely the imprint in the snowy slush of a half-worn rubber sole; and it was, of course, by no means certain that the sole belonged to the boot or shoe of the murderer of the two doomed women who had met so swift and awful a death in the arch near King's Cross station. The paper's special investigator pointed out that there were thousands of such soles being worn in London. Bunting found comfort in that obvious fact. He felt grateful to the special investigator for having stated it so clearly.

As he approached his house, he heard curious sounds coming from the inner side of the low wall that shut off the courtyard from the pavement. Under ordinary circumstances Bunting would have gone at once to drive whoever was there out into the roadway. Now he stayed outside, sick with suspense and anxiety. Was it possible that their place was being watched—already?

But it was only Mr Sleuth. To Bunting's astonishment, the lodger suddenly stepped forward from behind the wall on to the flagged path. He was carrying a brown-paper parcel, and, as he walked along, the new boots he was wearing creaked and the tap-tap of wooden heels rang out on the stones.

Bunting, still hidden outside the gate, suddenly understood what his lodger had been doing the other side of the wall, Mr Sleuth had been out to buy himself a pair of boots, and had gone inside the gate to put them on, placing his old footwear in the paper in which the new boots had been wrapped.

Bunting waited until Mr Sleuth had let himself into the house; then he also walked up the flagged pathway, and put his latch-key in the door.

In the next three days each of Bunting's waking hours held its mind of aching fear and suspense. From his point of view, almost any alternative would be preferable to that which to most people would have seemed the only one open to him. He told himself that it would be ruin for him and for his Ellen to be mixed up publicly in such a terrible affair. It would track them to their dying day.

Bunting was also always debating within himself as to whether he should tell Ellen of his frightful suspicion. He could not believe that what had become so plain to himself could long be concealed from all the world, and yet he did not credit his wife with the same intelligence. He did not even notice that, although she waited on Mr Sleuth as assiduously as ever, Mrs Bunting never mentioned the lodger.

Mr Sleuth, meanwhile, kept upstairs, he had given up going out altogether. He still felt, so he assured his landlady, far from well.

Daisy was another complication, the more so that the girl, whom her father longed to send away and whom he would hardly let out of his sight, showed herself inconveniently inquisitive concerning the lodger.

'Whatever does he do with himself all day?' she asked her stepmother.

'Well, just now he's reading the Bible,' Mrs Bunting had answered, very shortly and dryly.

'Well, I never! That's a funny thing for a gentleman to do!' Such had been Daisy's pert remark, and her stepmother had snubbed her well for it.

Daisy's eighteenth birthday dawned uneventfully. Her father gave her what he had always promised she should have on her eighteenth birthday—a watch. It was a pretty little silver watch, which Bunting had bought second-hand on the last day he had been happy; it seemed a long time ago now.

Mrs Bunting thought a silver watch was a very extravagant present, but she had always had the good sense not to interfere between her husband and his child. Besides, her mind was now full of other things. She was beginning to fear that Bunting suspected something, and she was filled with watchful anxiety and unease. What if he were to do anything silly—mix him up with the police, for instance? It certainly would be ruination to them both. But there—one never knew, with men! Her husband, however, kept his own counsel absolutely.

Daisy's birthday was a Saturday. In the middle of the morning Ellen and Daisy went down into the kitchen. Bunting didn't like the feeling that there was only one flight of stairs between Mr Sleuth and himself, so he quietly slipped out of the house and went to buy himself an ounce of tobacco.

In the last four days Bunting had avoided his usual haunts. But today the unfortunate man had a curious longing for human companionship—companionship, that is, other than that of Ellen and Daisy. This feeling led him into a small, populous thoroughfare hard by the Edgeware Road. There were more people there than usual, for the housewives of the neighbourhood were doing their marketing for Sunday.

Bunting passed the time of day with the tobacconist, and the two fell into desultory talk. To the ex-butler's surprise, the man said nothing at all to him on the subject of which all the neighbourhood must still be talking.

And then, quite suddenly, while still standing by the counter, and before he had paid for the packet of tobacco he held in his hand, Bunting, through the open door, saw, with horrified surprise, that his wife was standing outside a green-grocer's shop just opposite. Muttering a word of apology, he rushed out of the shop and across the road.

'Ellen!' he gasped hoarsely. 'You've never gone and left my little girl alone in the house?'

Mrs Bunting's face went chalky white. 'I thought you were indoors,' she said. 'You *were* indoors. Whatever made you come out for, without first making sure I was there?'

Bunting made no answer; but, as they stared at each other in exasperated silence, *each knew that the other knew*.

They turned and scurried down the street.

'Don't run,' he said suddenly; 'we shall get there just as quickly if we walk fast. People are noticing you, Ellen. Don't run.'

He spoke breathlessly, but it was breathlessness induced by fear and excitement, not by the quick pace at which they were walking.

As last they reached their own gate. Bunting pushed past in front of his wife. After all, Daisy was his child—Ellen couldn't know how he was feeling. He made the path almost in one leap, and fumbled for a moment with his latch-key. The door opened.

'Daisy!' he called out in a wailing voice. 'Daisy, my dear, where are you?'

'Here I am, father; what is it?'

'She's all right!' Bunting turned his grey face to his wife, 'She's all right, Ellen!' Then he waited a moment, leaning against the wall of the passage. 'It did give me a turn,' he said; and then, warningly, 'Don't frighten the girl, Ellen.'

Daisy was standing before the fire in the sitting-room, admiring herself in the glass. 'Oh, father,' she said, without turning round, 'I've seen the lodger! He's quite a nice gentleman—though, to be sure, he does look queer! He came down to ask Ellen for something, and we had quite a nice little chat. I told him it was my birthday, and he asked me to go to Madame Tussaud's with him this afternoon.' She laughed a little self-consciously. 'Of course I could see he was 'centric, and then at first he spoke so funnily. "And who be you?" he said, threatening-like. And I said to him, "I'm Mr Bunting's daughter, sir."

'"Then you're a very fortunate girl"—that's what he said, Ellen—"to 'ave such a nice stepmother as you've got. That's why," he said, "you look such a good, innocent girl." And then he quoted a bit of the prayer-book at me. "Keep innocency," he said, wagging his head at me. Lor'! It made me feel as if I was with aunt again.'

'I won't have you going out with the lodger—that's flat.' He was wiping his forehead with one hand, while with the other he mechanically squeezed the little packet of tobacco, for which, as he now remembered, he had forgotten to pay.

Daisy pouted. 'Oh, father, I think you might let me have a treat on my birthday! I told him Saturday wasn't a very good day—at least, so I'd heard—for Madame Tussaud's. Then he said we could go early, while the fine folk are still having their dinners. He wants you to come, too.' She turned to her stepmother, then giggled happily. 'The lodger has a wonderful fancy for you, Ellen; if I was father, I'd feel quite jealous!'

Her last words were cut across by a loud knock on the door. Bunting and his wife looked at each other apprehensively.

Both felt a curious thrill of relief when they saw that it was only Mr Sleuth—Mr Sleuth dressed to go out: the tall hat he had worn when he first came to them was in his hand, and he was wearing a heavy overcoat.

'I saw you had come in'—he addressed Mrs Bunting in his

high, whistling, hesitating voice, '—and so I've come down to ask if you and Miss Bunting will come to Madame Tussaud's now. I have never seen these famous waxworks, though I've heard of the place all my life.'

As Bunting forced himself to look fixedly at his lodger, a sudden doubt, bringing with it a sense of immeasurable relief, came to him. Surely it was inconceivable that this gentle, mild-mannered gentleman could be the monster of cruelty and cunning that Bunting had but a moment ago believed him to be!

'You're very kind, sir, I'm sure.' He tried to catch his wife's eye, but Mrs Bunting was looking away, staring into vacancy. She still, of course, wore the bonnet and cloak in which she had just been out to do her marketing. Daisy was already putting on her hat and coat.

Madame Tussaud's had hitherto held pleasant memories for Mrs Bunting. In the days when she and Bunting were courting they often spent part of their 'afternoon out' there. The butler had an acquaintance, a man named Hopkins, who was one of the waxworks' staff, and this man had sometimes given him passes for 'self and lady'. But this was the first time Mrs Bunting had been inside the place since she had come to live almost next door, as it were, to the big building.

The ill-sorted trio walked up the great staircase and into the first gallery; and there Mr Sleuth suddenly stopped short. The presence of those curious, still figures, suggesting death in life, seemed to surprise and affright him.

Daisy took quick advantage of the lodger's hesitation and unease.

'Oh, Ellen,' she cried, 'do let us begin by going into the Chamber of Horrors! I've never been in there. Aunt made father promise he wouldn't take me, the only time I've ever been here.

But now that I'm eighteen I can do just as I like; besides, aunt will never know!'

Mr Sleuth looked down at her.

'Yes,' he said, 'let us go into the Chamber of Horrors; that's a good idea, Miss Bunting.'

They turned into the great room in which the Napoleonic relics are kept, and which leads into the curious, vault-like chamber where waxen effigies of dead criminals stand grouped in wooden docks. Mrs Bunting was at once disturbed and relieved to see her husband's old acquaintance, Mr Hopkins, in charge of the turnstile admitting the public to the Chamber of Horrors.

'Well, you are a stranger,' the man observed genially. 'I do believe this is the very first time I've seen you in here, Mrs Bunting, since you married!'

'Yes,' she said; 'that is so. And this is my husband's daughter, Daisy; I expect you've heard of her, Mr Hopkins. And this,' she hesitated a moment, 'is our lodger, Mr Sleuth.'

But Mr Sleuth frowned and shuffled away. Daisy, leaving her stepmother's side, joined him.

Mrs Bunting put down three sixpences.

'Wait a minute,' said Hopkins; 'you can't go into the Chamber of Horrors just yet. But you won't have to wait more than four or five minutes, Mrs Bunting. It's this way, you see; our boss is in there, showing a party round.' He lowered his voice. 'It's Sir John Burney—I suppose you know who Sir John Burney is?'

'No,' she answered indifferently; 'I don't know that I ever heard of him.' She felt slightly—oh, very slightly—uneasy about Daisy. She would like her stepdaughter to keep well within sight and sound. Mr Sleuth was taking the girl to the other end of the room.

'Well, I hope you never *will* know him—not in any personal sense, Mrs Bunting.' The man chuckled. 'He's the Head Commissioner of Police—that's what Sir John Burney is. One of the gentlemen he's showing round our place is the Paris Prefect of Police, whose job is on all fours, so to speak, with Sir John's. The Frenchy has brought his daughter with him, and there are several other ladies. Ladies always like 'orrors, Mrs Bunting; that's our experience here. "Oh, take me to the Chamber of 'Orrors!"—that's what they say the minute they get into the building.'

A group of people, all talking and laughing together, were advancing from within toward the turnstile.

Mrs Bunting stared at them nervously. She wondered which of them was the gentleman with whom Mr Hopkins had hoped she would never be brought into personal contact. She quickly picked him out. He was a tall, powerful, nice-looking gentleman with a commanding manner. Just now he was smiling down into the face of a young lady. 'Monsieur Barberoux is quite right,' he was saying; 'the English law is too kind to the criminal, especially to the murderer. If we conducted our trials in the French fashion, the place we have just left would be very much fuller than it is today! A man of whose guilt we are absolutely assured is oftener than not acquitted, and then the public taunt us with "another undiscovered crime"!'

'D'you mean, Sir John, that murderers sometimes escape scot-free? Take the man who has been committing all those awful murders this last month.. Of course, I don't know much about it, for father won't let me read about it, but I can't help being interested!' Her girlish voice rang out, and Mrs Bunting heard every word distinctly.

The party gathered round, listening eagerly to hear what

the Head Commissioner would say next.

'Yes.' He spoke very deliberately. 'I think we may say—now, don't give me away to a newspaper fellow, Miss Rose—that we do know perfectly well who the murderer in question is—'

Several of those standing nearby uttered expressions of surprise and incredulity.

'Then why don't you catch him?' cried the girl indignantly.

'I didn't say we know where he is; I only said we know who he is; or, rather, perhaps I ought to say that we have a very strong suspicion of his identity.'

Sir John's French colleague looked up quickly. 'The Hamburg and Liverpool man?' he said interrogatively.

The other nodded. 'Yes; I suppose you've had the case turned up?'

Then, speaking very quickly, as if he wished to dismiss the subject from his own mind and from that of his auditors, he went on:

'Two murders of the kind were committed eight years ago—one in Hamburg, the other just afterward in Liverpool, and there were certain peculiarities connected with the crimes which made it clear they were committed by the same hand. The perpetrator was caught, fortunately for us red-handed, just as he was leaving the house of his victim, for in Liverpool the murder was committed in a house. I myself saw the unhappy man—I say unhappy, for there is no doubt at all that he was mad,'—he hesitated, and added in a lower tone—'suffering from an acute form of religious mania. I myself saw him, at some length. But now comes the really interesting point. Just a month ago this criminal, lunatic as we must regard him, made his escape from the asylum where he was confined. He arranged the whole thing with extraordinary cunning and intelligence, and we should probably have caught him long ago were it not that he managed, when on his way out of the place, to annex a considerable sum of money in gold with which the wages of the staff were about to be paid.'

The Frenchman again spoke. 'Why have you not circulated a description?' he asked.

'We did that at once,' Sir John Burney smiled a little grimly,' but only among our own people. We dare not circulate the man's description among the general public. You see, we may be mistaken, after all.'

'That is not very probable!' The Frenchman smiled a satirical little smile.

A moment later the party were walking in Indian file through the turnstile, Sir John Burney leading the way.

Mrs Bunting looked straight before her. Even had she wished to do so, she had neither time nor power to warn her lodger of his danger.

Daisy and her companion were now coming down the room, bearing straight for the Head Commissioner of Police. In another moment Mr Sleuth and Sir John Burney would be face to face.

Suddenly Mr Sleuth swerved to one side. A terrible change came over his pale, narrow face; it became discomposed, livid with rage and terror.

But, to Mrs Bunting's relief—yes, to her inexpressible relief—Sir John Burney and his friends swept on. They passed by Mr Sleuth unconcernedly, unaware, or so it seemed to her, that there was anyone else in the room but themselves.

'Hurry up, Mrs Bunting,' said the turnstile-keeper; 'you and your friends will have the place all to yourselves.' From an official he had become a man, and it was the man in

Mr Hopkins that gallantly addressed pretty Daisy Bunting. 'It seems strange that a young lady like you should want to go in and see those 'orrible frights,' he said jestingly.

'Mrs Bunting, may I trouble you to come over here for a moment?' The words were hissed rather than spoken by Mr Sleuth's lips.

His landlady took a doubtful step forward.

'A last word with you, Mrs Bunting.' The lodger's face was still distorted with fear and passion. 'Do you think you'd escape the consequences of your hideous treachery? I trusted you, Mrs Bunting, and you betrayed me! But I am protected by a higher power, for I still have work to do. Your end will be bitter as wormwood and sharp as a two-edged sword. Your feet shall go down to death, and your steps take hold on hell.' Even while Mr Sleuth was uttering these strange, dreadful words, he was looking around, his eyes glancing this way and that, seeking a way of escape.

At last his eyes became fixed on a small placard placed above a curtain. 'Emergency Exit' was written there. Leaving his landlady's side, he walked over to the turnstile. He fumbled in his pocket for a moment, and then touched the man on the arm. 'I feel ill,' he said, speaking very rapidly; 'very ill indeed! It's the atmosphere of this place. I want you to let me out by the quickest way. It would be a pity for me to faint here—especially with ladies about.' His left hand shot out and placed what he had been fumbling for in his pocket on the other's bare palm. 'I see there's an emergency exit over there. Would it be possible for me to get out that way?'

'Well, yes, sir; I think so.' The man hesitated; he felt a slight, a very slight, feeling of misgiving. He looked at Daisy, flushed and smiling, happy and unconcerned, and then at Mrs Bunting.

She was very pale; but surely her lodger's sudden seizure was enough to make her feel worried. Hopkins felt the half-sovereign pleasantly tickling his paten. The Prefect of Police had given him only half a crown—mean, shabby foreigner!

'Yes, I can let you out that way,' he said at last, 'and perhaps when you're standing out in the air on the iron balcony you'll feel better. But then you know, sir, you'll have to come round to the front if you want to come in again, for those emergency doors only open outward.'

'Yes, yes,' said Mr Sleuth hurriedly; 'I quite understand! If I feel better I'll come in by the front way, and pay another shilling—that's only fair.'

'You needn't do that if you'll just explain what happened here.'

The man went and pulled the curtain aside, and put his shoulder against the door. It burst open, and the light for a moment blinded Mr Sleuth. He passed his hand over his eyes.

'Thank you,' he said; 'thank you. I shall get all right here.'

Five days later Bunting identified the body of a man found drowned in the Regent's Canal as that of his late lodger; and, the morning following, a gardener working in the Regent's Park found a newspaper in which were wrapped, together with a half-worn pair of rubber-soled shoes, two surgical knives. This fact was not chronicled in any newspaper; but a very pretty and picturesque paragraph went the round of the press, about the same time, concerning a small box filled with sovereigns which had been forwarded anonymously to the Governor of the Foundling Hospital.

Mr and Mrs Bunting are now in the service of an old lady, by whom they are feared as well as respected, and whom they make very comfortable.

THE DUEL

Wilkie Collins

The doctors could do no more for the dowager Lady Berrick. When the medical advisers of a lady who has reached seventy years of age recommend the mild climate of the South of France, they mean in plain language that they have arrived at the end of their resources. Her ladyship gave the mild climate a fair trial, and then decided (as she herself expressed it) to 'die at home'. Travelling slowly, she had reached Paris at the date when I last heard of her. It was then the beginning of November. A week later, I met with her nephew, Lewis Romayne, at the club.

'What brings you to London at this time of the year?' I asked.

'The fatality that pursues me,' he answered grimly. 'I am one of the unluckiest men living.'

He was thirty years old; he was not married; he was the enviable possessor of the tiny old country seat, called Vange Abbey; he had no poor relations; and he was one of the handsomest men in England. When I add that I am, myself, a retired army officer, with a wretched income, a disagreeable wife, four ugly children, and a burden of fifty years on my back, no one will be surprised to hear that I answered Romayne, with bitter sincerity, in these words:

'I wish to Heaven I could change places with you!'

'I wish to Heaven you could!' he burst out, with equal sincerity on his side. 'Read that.'

He handed me a letter addressed to him by the travelling medical attendant of Lady Berrick. After resting in Paris, the patient had continued her homeward journey as far as Boulogne. In her suffering condition, she was liable to sudden fits of caprice. An insurmountable horror of the Channel passage had got possession of her: she positively refused to be taken on board the steamboat. In this difficulty, the lady who held the post of her 'companion' had ventured on a suggestion. Would Lady Berrick consent to make the Channel passage if her nephew came to Boulogne expressly to accompany her on the voyage? The reply had been so immediately favourable, that the doctor lost no time in communicating with Mr Lewis Romayne. This was the substance of the letter.

It was needless to ask any more questions—Romayne was plainly on his way to Boulogne. I gave him some useful information. 'Try the oysters,' I said, 'at the restaurant on the pier.'

He never even thanked me. He was thinking entirely of himself.

'Just look at my position,' he said. 'I detest Boulogne; I cordially share my aunt's horror of the Channel passage; I had looked forward to some months of happy retirement in the country among my books—and what happens to me? I am brought to London in this season of fogs, to travel by the tidal train at seven tomorrow morning—and all for a woman with whom I have no sympathies in common. If I am not an unlucky man—who is?'

He spoke in a tone of vehement irritation which seemed

to me, under the circumstances, to be simply absurd. But *my* nervous system is not the irritable system—sorely tried by night study and strong tea—of my friend Romayne. 'It's only a matter of two days,' I remarked, by way of reconciling him to his situation.

'How do I know that?' he retorted. 'In two days the weather may be stormy. In two days she may be too ill to be moved. Unfortunately, I am her heir; and I am told I must submit to any whim that seizes her. I'm rich enough already; I don't want her money. Besides, I dislike all travelling—and especially travelling alone. You are an idle man. If you were a good friend, you would offer to go with me.' He added, with the delicacy which was one of the redeeming points in his wayward character, 'Of course as my guest.'

I had known him long enough not to take offence at his reminding me, in this considerate way, that I was a poor man. The proposed change of scene tempted me. What did I care for the Channel passage? Besides, there was the irresistible attraction of getting away from home.

The end of it was that I accepted Romayne's invitation.

II

Shortly after noon, on the next day, we were established at Boulogne—near Lady Berrick, but not at her hotel. 'If we live in the same house,' Romayne reminded me, 'we shall be bored by the companion and the doctor. Meetings on the stairs, you know, and exchanging bows and small talk.' He hated those trivial conventionalities of society, in which other people delight. When somebody once asked him in what company he felt most at ease? He made a shocking answer—he said, 'In the company of dogs.'

I waited for him on the pier while he went to see her ladyship. He joined me again with his bitterest smile. 'What did I tell you? She is not well enough to see me today. The doctor looks grave, and the companion puts her handkerchief to her eyes. We may be kept in this place for weeks to come.'

The afternoon proved to be rainy. Our early dinner was a bad one. This last circumstance tried his temper sorely. He was no gourmand; the question of cookery was (with him) purely a matter of digestion. Those late hours of study and that abuse of tea to which I have already alluded, had sadly injured his stomach. The doctors warned him of serious consequences to his nervous system, unless he altered his habits. He had little faith in medical science, and he greatly overrated the restorative capacity of his constitution. So far as I know, he had always neglected the doctors' advice.

The weather cleared towards evening, and we went out for a walk. We passed a church—a Roman Catholic church, of course—the doors of which were still open. Some poor women were kneeling at their prayers in the dim light. 'Wait a minute,' said Romayne. 'I am in a vile temper. Let me try to put myself into a better frame of mind.'

I followed him into the church. He knelt down in a dark corner by himself. I confess I was surprised. He had been baptized in the Church of England; but, so far as outward practice was concerned, he belonged to no religious community. I had often heard him speak with sincere reverence and admiration of the spirit of Christianity—but he never, to my knowledge, attended any place of public worship. When we met again outside the church, I asked if he had been converted to the Roman Catholic faith.

'No,' he said. 'I hate the inveterate striving of that priesthood after social influence and political power as cordially as the fiercest Protestant living. But let us not forget that the Church of Rome has great merits to set against great faults. Its system is administered with an admirable knowledge of the higher needs of human nature. Take as one example what you have just seen. The solemn tranquillity of that church, the poor people praying near me, the few words of prayer by which I silently united myself to my fellow creatures have calmed me, and done me good. In our country I should have found the church closed, out-of-service hours.' He took my arm, and abruptly changed the subject. 'How will you occupy yourself,' he asked, 'if my aunt receives me tomorrow?'

I assured him that I should easily find ways and means of getting through the time. The next morning a message came from Lady Berrick, to say that she would see her nephew after breakfast. Left by myself, I walked towards the pier, and met with a man who asked me to hire his boat. He had lines and bait, at my service. Most unfortunately, as the event proved, I decided on occupying an hour or two by sea fishing.

The wind shifted while we were out, and before we could get back to the harbour, the tide had turned against us. It was six o'clock when I arrived at the hotel. A little open carriage was waiting at the door. I found Romayne impatiently expecting me, and no signs of dinner on the table. He informed me that he had accepted an invitation, in which I was included, and promised to explain everything in the carriage.

Our driver took the road that led towards the High Town. I subordinated my curiosity to my sense of politeness, and asked for news of his aunt's health.

'She is seriously ill, poor soul,' he said. 'I am sorry I spoke so petulantly and so unfairly when we met at the club. The near prospect of death has developed qualities in her nature which I ought to have seen before this. No matter how it may be delayed, I will patiently wait her time for the crossing to England.'

So long as he believed himself to be in the right, he was, as to his actions and opinions, one of the most obstinate men I ever met with. But once let him be convinced that he was wrong, and he rushed into the other extreme—became needlessly distrustful of himself, and needlessly eager in seizing his opportunity of making atonement. In this latter mood he was capable (with the best intentions) of committing acts of the most childish imprudence. With some misgivings, I asked how he had amused himself in my absence.

'I waited for you,' he said, 'till I lost all patience, and went out for a walk. First, I thought of going to the beach, but the smell of the harbour drove me back into the town; and there, oddly enough, I met with a man, a certain Captain Peterkin, who had been a friend of mine at college.'

'A visitor to Boulogne?' I inquired.

'Not exactly.'

'A resident?'

'Yes. The fact is, I lost sight of Peterkin when I left Oxford—and since that time he seems to have drifted into difficulties. We had a long talk. He is living here, he tells me, until his affairs are settled.'

I needed no further enlightenment—Captain Peterkin stood as plainly revealed to me as if I had known him for years. 'Isn't it a little imprudent,' I said, 'to renew your acquaintance with a man of that sort? Couldn't you have passed him, with a bow?'

Romayne smiled uneasily. 'I dare say you're right,' he answered, 'But, remember, I had left my aunt, feeling ashamed of the unjust way in which I had thought and spoken of her. How did I know that I mightn't be wronging an old friend next, if I kept Peterkin at a distance? His present position may be as much his misfortune, poor fellow, as his fault. I was half inclined to pass him, as you say—but I distrusted my own judgement. He held out his hand, and he was so glad to see me. It can't be helped now. I shall be anxious to hear your opinion of him.'

'Are we going to dine with Captain Peterkin?'

'Yes. I happened to mention that wretched dinner yesterday at our hotel. He said, "Come to my boarding-house. Out of Paris, there isn't such a table d'hote in France." I tried to get off it not caring, as you know, to go among strangers—I said I had a friend with me. He invited you most cordially to accompany me. More excuses on my part only led to a painful result. I hurt Peterkin's feelings. "I'm down in the world," he said, "and I'm not fit company for you and your friends. I beg your pardon for taking the liberty of inviting you!" He turned away with tears in his eyes. What could I do?'

I thought to myself, 'You could have lent him five pounds, and got rid of his invitation without the slightest difficulty.' If I had returned in reasonable time to go out with Romayne, we might not have met the captain—or, if we had met him, my presence would have prevented the confidential talk and the invitation that followed. I felt I was to blame—and yet, how could I help it? It was useless to remonstrate: the mischief was done.

We left the Old Town on our right hand, and drove on, past a little colony of suburban villas, to a house standing by itself, surrounded by a stone wall. As we crossed the front garden on our way to the door, I noticed against the side of the house two kennels, inhabited by two large watch-dogs. Was the proprietor afraid of thieves?

III

The moment we were introduced to the drawing-room, my suspicions of the company we were likely to meet with were fully confirmed.

'Cards, billiards, and betting'—there was the inscription legibly written on the manner and appearance of Captain Peterkin. The bright-eyed yellow old lady who kept the boarding-house would have been worth five thousand pounds in jewellery alone, if the ornaments which profusely covered her had been genuine precious stones. The younger ladies present had their cheeks as highly rouged and their eyelids as elaborately pencilled in black as if they were going on the stage, instead of going to dinner. We found these fair creatures drinking Madeira as a whet to their appetites. Among the men, there were two who struck me as the most finished and complete blackguards whom I had ever met within all my experience, at home and abroad. One, with a brown face and a broken nose, was presented to us by the title of 'Commander', and was described as a person of great wealth and distinction in Peru, travelling for amusement. The other wore a military uniform and decorations, and was spoken of as 'the General.' A bold bullying manner, a fat sodden face, little leering eyes, and greasy-looking hands, made this man so repellent to me that I privately longed to kick him. Romayne had evidently been announced, before our arrival, as a landed gentleman with a large income. Men and women vied in servile attentions to him. When we went into the dining-room, the fascinating creature who sat next to him held her fan before her face, and so made a private interview of it between the rich Englishman and herself. With regard to the dinner, I shall only report that it justified Captain Peterkin's boast, in some degree at least. The wine was good, and the conversation became gay to the verge of indelicacy. Usually the most temperate of men, Romayne was tempted by his neighbours into drinking freely. I was unfortunately seated at the opposite extremity of the table, and I had no opportunity of warning him.

The dinner reached its conclusion, and we all returned together, on the foreign plan, to coffee and cigars in the drawing-room. The women smoked, and drank liqueurs as well as coffee, with the men. One of them went to the piano, and a little impromptu ball followed, the ladies dancing with their cigarettes in their mouths. Keeping my eyes and ears on the alert, I saw an innocent-looking table, with a surface of rosewood, suddenly develop a substance of green cloth. At the same time, a neat little roulette-table made its appearance from a hiding-place in a sofa. Passing near the venerable landlady, I heard her ask the servant, in a whisper, 'if the dogs were loose?' After what I had observed, I could only conclude that the dogs were used as a patrol, to give the alarm in case of a descent of the police. It was plainly high time to thank Captain Peterkin for his hospitality, and to take our leave.

'We have had enough of this,' I whispered to Romayne in English. 'Let us go.'

In these days it is a delusion to suppose that you can speak confidentially in the English language, when French people are within hearing. One of the ladies asked Romayne, tenderly, if he was tired of her already. Another reminded him that it was raining heavily (as we could all hear), and suggested waiting until it it cleared up. The hideous General waved his greasy hand in the direction of the card table, and said, 'The game is waiting for us.'

Romayne was excited, but not stupefied, by the wine he

had drunk. He answered, discreetly enough, 'I must beg you to excuse me; I am a poor card player.'

The General suddenly looked gave. 'You are speaking, sir, under a strange misapprehension,' he said. 'Our game is lansquenet—essentially a game of chance. With luck, the poorest player is a match for the whole table.'

Romayne persisted in his refusal. As a matter of course, I supported him, with all needful care to avoid giving offence. The General took offence, nevertheless. He crossed his arms on his breast, and looked at us fiercely.

'Does this mean, gentlemen, that you distrust the company?' he asked.

The broken-nosed Commander, hearing the question, immediately joined us, in the interests of peace-bearing with him the elements of persuasion, under the form of a lady on his arm.

The lady stepped briskly forward, and tapped the General on the shoulder with her fan. 'I am one of the company,' she said, 'and I am sure Mr Romayne doesn't distrust *me*.' She turned to Romayne with her most irresistible smile. 'A gentleman always plays cards,' she resumed, 'when he has a lady for a partner. Let us join our interests at the table—and, dear Mr Romayne, don't risk too much!' She put her pretty little purse into his hand, and looked as if she had been in love with him for half her lifetime.

The fatal influence of the sex, assisted by wine, produced the inevitable result. Romayne allowed himself to be led to the card table. For a moment the General delayed the beginning of the game. After what had happened, it was necessary that he should assert the strict sense of justice that was in him. 'We are all honourable men,' he began.

'And brave men,' the Commander added, admiring the General.

'And brave men,' the General admitted, admiring the Commander. 'Gentlemen, if I have been led into expressing myself with unnecessary warmth of feeling, I apologize, and regret it.'

'Nobly spoken!' the Commander pronounced. The General put his hand on his heart and bowed. The game began.

As the poorest man of the two, I had escaped the attentions lavished by the ladies on Romayne. At the same time, I was obliged to pay for my dinner, by taking some part in the proceedings of the evening. Small stakes were allowed, I found, at roulette; and, besides, the heavy chances in favour of the table made it hardly worth while to run the risk of cheating in this case. I placed myself next to the least rascally-looking man in the company, and played roulette.

For a wonder, I was successful at the first attempt. My neighbour handed me my winnings. 'I have lost every farthing I possess,' he whispered to me, piteously, 'and I have a wife and children at home.' I lent the poor wretch five francs. He smiled faintly as he looked at the money. 'It reminds me,' he said, 'of my last transaction, when I borrowed of that gentleman there, who is betting on the General's luck at the card table. Beware of employing him as I did. What do you think I got for my note of hand of four thousand francs? A hundred bottles of champagne, fifty bottles of ink, fifty bottles of blacking, three dozen handkerchiefs, two pictures by unknown masters, two shawls, one hundred maps, *and*—five francs.'

'We went on playing. My luck deserted tile; I lost, and lost, and lost again. From time to time I looked round at the card table. The 'deal' had fallen early to the General, and it seemed to be indefinitely prolonged. A heap of notes and gold (won mainly from Romayne, as I afterwards discovered) lay before him. As for my neighbour, the unhappy possessor of the bottles of blacking, the pictures by unknown masters, and the rest of it, he won, and then rashly presumed on his good fortune. Deprived of his last farthing, he retired into a corner of the room, and consoled himself with a cigar. I had just risen, to follow his example, when a furious uproar burst out at the card table.

I saw Romayne spring up, and snatch the cards out of the General's hand. 'You scoundrel!' he shouted, 'you are cheating!' The General started to his feet in a fury. 'You lie!' he cried. I attempted to interfere, but Romayne had already seen the necessity of controlling himself. 'A gentleman doesn't accept an insult from a swindler,' he said coolly. 'Accept this, then!' the General answered—and spat on him. In an instant Romayne knocked him down.

The blow was dealt straight between his eyes: he was a gross big-boned man, and he fell heavily. For the time he was stunned. The women ran, screaming, out of the room. The peaceable Commander trembled from head to foot. Two of the men present, who, to give them their due, were no cowards, locked the doors. 'You don't go,' they said, 'till we see whether he recovers or not.' Cold water, assisted by the landlady's smelling salts, brought the General to his senses after a while. He whispered something to one of his friends, who immediately turned to me. 'The General challenges Mr Romayne,' he said. 'As one of his seconds, I demand an appointment for tomorrow morning.' I refused to make any appointment unless the doors were first unlocked, and we were left free to depart. 'Our carriage is waiting outside,' I added. 'If it returns to the hotel without us, there will be an inquiry.' This latter consideration had its effect. On their side, the doors were opened. On our side, the appointment was made. We left the house.

V

We were punctual to the appointed hour—eight o'clock.

The second who acted with me was a French gentleman, a relative of one of the officers who had brought the challenge. At his suggestion, we had chosen the pistol as our weapon. Romayne, like most Englishmen at the present time, knew nothing of the use of the sword. He was almost equally inexperienced with the pistol.

Our opponents were late. They kept us waiting for more than ten minutes. It was not pleasant weather to wait in. The day had dawned damp and drizzling. A thick white fog was slowly rolling in on us from the sea.

When they did appear, the General was not among them. A tall, well-dressed young man saluted Romayne with stern courtesy, and said to a stranger who accompanied him, 'Explain the circumstances.'

The stranger proved to be a surgeon. He entered at once on the necessary explanation. The General was too ill to appear. He had been attacked that morning by a fit—the consequence of the blow that he had received. Under these circumstances, his eldest son (Maurice) was now on the ground to fight the duel, on his father's behalf; attended by the General's seconds, and with the General's full approval.

We instantly refused to allow the duel to take place, Romayne loudly declaring that he had no quarrel with the General's son. Upon this, Maurice broke away from his seconds; drew off one of his gloves; and stepping close up to Romayne, struck him on the face with the glove. 'Have you no quarrel with me now?' the young Frenchman asked. 'Must I spit on you, as my father did?' His seconds dragged him away, and apologized to us for the outbreak. But the mischief was done. Romayne's fiery temper flashed in his eyes. 'Load the pistols,' he said. After the insult publicly offered to him, and the outrage publicly threatened, there was no other course to take.

It had been left to us to produce the pistols. We therefore requested the seconds of our opponent to examine, and to load them. While this was being done, the advancing sea-fog so completely enveloped us, that the duelists were unable to see each other. We were obliged to wait for the chance of a partial clearing in the atmosphere. Romayne's temper had become calm again. The generosity of his nature spoke in the words which he now addressed to his seconds.

'After all,' he said, 'the young man is a good son—he is bent on redressing what he believes to be his father's wrong. Does his flipping his glove in my face matter to me? I think I shall fire in the air.'

'I shall refuse to act as your second if you do,' answered the French gentleman who was assisting us. 'The General's son is famous for his skill with the pistol. If you didn't see it in his face just now, I did—he means to kill you. Defend your life, sir!' I spoke quite as strongly, to the same purpose, when my turn came. Romayne yielded—he placed himself unreservedly in our hands.

In a quarter of an hour the fog lifted a little. We measured the distance, having previously arranged (at my suggestion) that the two men should both fire at the same moment, at a given signal. Romayne's composure, as they faced each other, was, in a man of his irritable nervous temperament, really wonderful. I placed him sideways, in a position which in some degree lessened his danger, by lessening the surface exposed to the bullet. My French colleague put the pistol into his hand, and gave him the last word of advice. 'Let your arm hang loosely down, with the barrel of the pistol pointing straight to the ground. When you hear the signal, only lift your arm as far as the elbow; keep the elbow pressed against your side—and fire.' We could do no more for him. As we drew aside—I own it—my tongue was like a cinder in my mouth, and a horrid inner cold crept through me to the marrow of my bones.

The signal was given, and the two shots were fired at the same time.

My first look was at Romayne. He took off his hat, and handed it to me with a smile. His adversary's bullet had cut a piece out of the brim of his hat, on the right side. He had literally escaped by a hairbreadth.

While I was congratulating him, the fog gathered again more thickly than ever. Looking anxiously towards the ground occupied by our adversaries, we could only see vague, shadowy forms hurriedly crossing and re-crossing each other in the mist. Something had happened! My French colleague took my arm and pressed it significantly. 'Leave me to inquire,' he said. Romayne tried to follow; I held him back, neither of us exchanged a word.

The fog thickened and thickened, until nothing was to be seen. Once we heard the surgeon's voice, calling impatiently for a light to help him. No light appeared that we could see. Dreary as the fog itself, the silence gathered round us again. On a sudden broken, horribly broken, by another voice, strange to both it was one of us, shrieking hysterically through the impenetrable mist. 'Where is he?' the voice cried, in the French language.

'Assassin! Assassin! Where are you?' Was it a woman? or was it a boy? We heard nothing more. The effect upon Romayne was terrible to see. He who had calmly confronted the weapon lifted to kill him, shuddered dumbly like a terror-stricken animal. I put my arm round him, and hurried him away from the place.

We waited at the hotel until our French friend joined us. After a brief interval he appeared, announcing that the surgeon would follow him.

The duel had ended fatally. The chance course of the bullet, urged by Romayne's unpractised hand, had struck the General's son just above the right nostril—had penetrated to the back of his neck—and had communicated a fatal shock to the spinal marrow. He was a dead man before they could take him back to his father's house.

So far, our fears were confirmed. But there was something else to tell, for which our worst presentiments had not prepared us.

A younger brother of the fallen man (a boy of thirteen years old) had secretly followed the duelling party, on their way from his father's house—had hidden himself—and had seen the dreadful end. The seconds only knew of it when he burst out of his place of concealment, and fell on his knees by his dying brother's side. His were the frightful cries which we had heard from invisible lips. The slayer of his brother was the 'assassin' whom he had vainly tried to discover through the fathomless obscurity of the mist.

We both looked at Romayne. He silently looked back at us, like a man turned to stone. I tried to reason with him.

'Your life was at your opponent's mercy,' I said. 'It was *he* who was skilled in the use of the pistol; your risk was infinitely greater than his. Are you responsible for an accident? Rouse yourself, Romayne! Think of the time to come, when all this will be forgotten.'

'Never,' he said, 'to the end of my life.'

He made that reply in dull monotonous tones. His eyes looked wearily and vacantly straight before him. I spoke to him again. He remained impenetrably silent; he appeared not to hear, or not to understand me. The surgeon came in, while I was still at a loss what to say or do next. Without waiting to be asked for his opinion, he observed Romayne attentively, and then drew me away into the next room.

'Your friend is suffering from a severe nervous shock,' he said. 'Can you tell me anything of his habits of life?'

I mentioned the prolonged night studies, and the excessive use of tea. The surgeon shook his head.

'If you want my advice,' he proceeded, 'take him home at once. Don't subject him to further excitement, when the result of the duel is known in the town. If it ends in our appearing in a court of law, it will be a mere formality in this case, and you can surrender when the time comes. Leave me your address in London.'

I felt that the wisest thing I could do was to follow his advice. The boat crossed to Folkestone at an early hour that day—we had no time to lose. Romayne offered no objection to our return to England; he seemed perfectly careless of what became of him. 'Leave me quiet,' he said: 'and do as you like.' I wrote a few lines to Lady Berrick's medical attendant, informing him of the circumstances. A quarter of an hour afterwards we were on board the steamboat.

THE CASK OF AMONTILLADO

Edgar Allan Poe

The thousand injuries of Fortunato I had borne as I best could, but when he ventured upon insult, I vowed revenge. You, who so well know the nature of my soul, will not suppose, however, that I gave utterance to a threat. *At length* I would be avenged; this was a point definitely settled—but the very definitiveness with which it was resolved, precluded the idea of risk. I must not only punish, but punish with impunity. A wrong is unredressed when retribution overtakes its redresser. It is equally unredressed when the avenger fails to make himself felt as such to him who has done the wrong.

It must be understood that neither by word nor deed had I given Fortunato cause to doubt my good will. I continued, as was my wont, to smile in his face, and he did not perceive that my smile *now* was at the thought of his immolation.

He had a weak point—this Fortunato—although in other regards he was a man to be respected and even feared. He prided himself on his connoisseurship in wine. Few Italians have the true virtuoso spirit. For the most part their enthusiasm is adopted to suit the time and opportunity—to practise imposture upon the British and Austrian *millionaires*. In painting and gemmary, Fortunato, like his countrymen, was a quack—but in the matter of old wines he was sincere. In this respect I did not differ from him materially: I was skilful in the Italian vintages myself, and bought largely whenever I could.

It was about dusk, one evening during the supreme madness of the carnival season, that I encountered my friend. He accosted me with excessive warmth, for he had been drinking much. The man wore motley. He had on a tight-fitting parti-striped dress, and his head was surmounted by the conical cap and bells. I was so pleased to see him, that I thought I should never have done wringing his hand.

I said to him—'My dear Fortunato, you are luckily met. How remarkably well you are looking today! But I have received a pipe of what passes for Amontillado, and I have my doubts.'

'How?' said he. 'Amontillado? A pipe? Impossible! And in the middle of the carnival!'

'I have my doubts,' I replied; 'and I was silly enough to pay the full Amontillado price without consulting you in the matter. You were not to be found, and I was fearful of losing a bargain.'

'Amontillado!'

'I have my doubts.'

'Amontillado!'

'And I must satisfy them.'

'Amontillado!'

'As you are engaged, I am on my way to Luchesi. If any one has a critical turn, it is he. He will tell me—'

'Luchesi cannot tell Amontillado from Sherry.'

'And yet some fools will have it that his taste is a match for your own.'

'Come, let us go.'

'Whither?'

'To your vaults.'

'My friend, no; I will not impose upon your good nature. I perceive you have an engagement. Luchesi—'

'I have no engagement;—come.'

'My friend, no. It is not the engagement, but the severe cold with which I perceive you are afflicted. The vaults are insufferably damp. They are encrusted with nitre.'

'Let us go, nevertheless. The cold is merely nothing. Amontillado! You have been imposed upon. And as for Luchesi, he cannot distinguish Sherry from Amontillado.'

Thus speaking, Fortunato possessed himself of my arm. Putting on a mask of black silk, and drawing a *roquelaire* closely about my person, I suffered him to hurry me to my palazzo.

There were no attendants at home; they had absconded to make merry in honour of the time. I had told them that I should not return until the morning, and had given them explicit orders not to stir from the house. These orders were sufficient, I well knew, to insure their immediate disappearance, one and all, as soon as my back was turned.

I took from their sconces two flambeaux, and giving one to Fortunato, bowed him through several suites of rooms to the archway that led into the vaults. I passed down a long and winding staircase, requesting him to be cautious as he followed. We came at length to the foot of the descent, and stood together on the damp ground of the catacombs of the Montresors.

The gait of my friend was unsteady, and the bells upon his cap jingled as he strode.

'The pipe,' said he.

'It is farther on,' said I; 'but observe the white web-work which gleams from these cavern walls.'

He turned towards me, and looked into my eyes with two

filmy orbs that distilled the rheum of intoxication.

'Nitre?' he asked, at length.

'Nitre,' I replied. 'How long have you had that cough?'

'Ugh! ugh! ugh!—ugh! ugh! ugh!—ugh! ugh! ugh!—ugh! ugh!—ugh! ugh! ugh!'

My poor friend found it impossible to reply for many minutes.

'It is nothing,' he said, at last.

'Come,' I said, with decision, 'we will go back; your health is precious. You are rich, respected, admired, beloved; you are happy, as once I was. You are a man to be missed. For me it is no matter. We will go back; you will be ill, and I cannot be responsible. Besides, there is Luchesi—'

'Enough,' he said; 'the cough is a mere nothing; it will not kill me. I shall not die of a cough.'

'True—true,' I replied; 'and, indeed, I had no intention of alarming you unnecessarily—but you should use all proper caution. A draught of this Medoc will defend us from the damps.'

Here I knocked off the neck of a bottle which I drew from a long row of its fellows that lay upon the mould.

'Drink,' I said, presenting him the wine.

He raised it to his lips with a leer. He paused and nodded to me familiarly, while his bells jingled.

'I drink,' he said, 'to the buried that repose around us.'

'And I to your long life.'

He again took my arm, and we proceeded.

'These vaults,' he said, 'are extensive.'

'The Montresors,' I replied, 'were a great and numerous family.'

'I forget your arms.'

'A huge human foot d'or, in a field azure; the foot crushes

a serpent rampant whose fangs are imbedded in the heel.'

'And the motto?'

'*Nemo me impune lacessit.*'

'Good!' he said.

The wine sparkled in his eyes and the bells jingled. My own fancy grew warm with the Medoc. We had passed through walls of piled bones, with casks and puncheons intermingling, into the inmost recesses of catacombs. I paused again, and this time I made bold to seize Fortunato by an arm above the elbow.

'The nitre!' I said; 'see, it increases. It hangs like moss upon the vaults. We are below the river's bed. The drops of moisture trickle among the bones. Come, we will go back ere it is too late. Your cough—'

'It is nothing,' he said; 'let us go on. But first, another draught of the Medoc.'

I broke and reached him a flagon of De Grave. He emptied it at a breath. His eyes flashed with a fierce light. He laughed and threw the bottle upwards with a gesticulation I did not understand.

I looked at him in surprise. He repeated the movement—a grotesque one.

'You do not comprehend?' he said.

'Not I,' I replied.

'Then you are not of the brotherhood.'

'How?'

'You are not of the masons.'

'Yes, yes,' I said; 'yes, yes.'

'You? Impossible! A mason?'

'A mason,' I replied.

'A sign,' he said, 'a sign'.

'It is this,' I answered, producing a trowel from beneath

the folds of my *roquelaire*.

'You jest,' he exclaimed, recoiling a few paces. 'But let us proceed to the Amontillado.'

'Be it so,' I said, replacing the tool beneath the cloak and again offering him my arm. He leaned upon it heavily. We continued our route in search of the Amontillado. We passed through a range of low arches, descended, passed on, and descending again, arrived at a deep crypt, in which the foulness of the air caused our flambeaux rather to glow than flame.

At the most remote end of the crypt there appeared another less spacious one. Its walls had been lined with human remains, piled to the vault overhead, in the fashion of the great catacombs of Paris. Three sides of this interior crypt were still ornamented in this manner. From the fourth side the bones had been thrown down, and lay promiscuously upon the earth, forming at one point a mound of some size. Within the wall thus exposed by the displacing of the bones, we perceived a still interior recess, in depth about four feet, in width three, in height six or seven. It seemed to have been constructed for no especial use within itself, but formed merely the interval between two of the colossal supports of the roof of the catacombs, and was backed by one of their circumscribing walls of solid granite.

It was in vain that Fortunato, uplifting his dull torch, endeavoured to pry into the depth of the recess. Its termination the feeble light did not enable us to see.

'Proceed,' I said; 'herein is the Amontillado. As for Luchesi—'

'He is an ignoramus,' interrupted my friend, as he stepped unsteadily forward, while I followed immediately at his heels. In an instant he had reached the extremity of the niche, and finding his progress arrested by the rock, stood stupidly bewildered. A moment more and I had fettered him to the granite. In its surface were two iron staples, distant from each other about two feet, horizontally. From one of these depended a short chain, from the other a padlock. Throwing the links about his waist, it was but the work of a few seconds to secure it. He was too much astounded to resist. Withdrawing the key I stepped back from the recess.

'Pass your hand,' I said, 'over the wall; you cannot help feeling the nitre. Indeed, it is *very* damp. Once more let me *implore* you to return. No? Then I must positively leave you. But I must first render you all the little attentions in my power.'

'The Amontillado!' ejaculated my friend, not yet recovered from his astonishment.

'True,' I replied; 'the Amontillado.'

As I said these words I busied myself among the pile of bones of which I have before spoken. Throwing them aside, I soon uncovered a quantity of building stone and mortar. With these materials and with the aid of my trowel, I began vigorously to wall up the entrance of the niche.

I had scarcely laid the first tier of the masonry when I discovered that the intoxication of Fortunato had in a great measure worn off. The earliest indication I had of this was a low moaning cry from the depth of the recess. It was *not* the cry of a drunken man. There was then a long and obstinate silence. I laid the second tier, and the third, and the fourth; and then I heard the furious vibrations of the chain. The noise lasted for several minutes, during which, that I might hearken to it with the more satisfaction, I ceased my labours and sat down upon the bones. When at last the clanking subsided, I resumed the trowel, and finished without interruption the fifth, the sixth, and the seventh tier. The wall was now nearly upon a level with my breast. I again paused, and holding the flambeaux over the mason-work, threw a few feeble rays upon the figure within.

A succession of loud and shrill screams, bursting suddenly from the throat of the chained form, seemed to thrust me violently back. For a brief moment I hesitated—I trembled. Unsheathing my rapier, I began to grope with it about the recess; but the thought of an instant reassured me. I placed my hand upon the solid fabric of the catacombs, and felt satisfied. I reapproached the wall; I replied to the yells of him who clamoured. I re-echoed—I aided—I surpassed them in volume and in strength. I did this, and the clamourer grew still.

It was now midnight, and my task was drawing to a close. I had completed the eighth, the ninth, and the tenth tier. I had finished a portion of the last and the eleventh; there remained but a single stone to be fitted and plastered in. I struggled with its weight; I placed it partially in its destined position. But now there came from out the niche a low laugh that erected the hair upon my head. It was succeeded by a sad voice, which I had difficulty in recognizing as that of the noble Fortunato. The voice said—

'Ha! ha! ha!—he! he! he!—a very good joke indeed—an excellent jest. We shall have many a rich laugh about it at the palazzo—he! he! he!—over our wine—he! he! he!'

'The Amontillado!' I said.

'He! he! he!—he! he! he!—yes, the Amontillado. But is it not getting late? Will not they be awaiting us at the palazzo, the Lady Fortunato and the rest? Let us be gone.'

'Yes,' I said, 'let us be gone.'

'For the love of God, Montresor!'

'Yes,' I said, 'for the love of God!'

But to these words I hearkened in vain for a reply. I grew impatient. I called aloud—

'Fortunato!'

No answer. I called again—

'Fortunato—'

No answer still. I thrust a torch through the remaining aperture and let it fall within. There came forth in reply only a jingling of the bells. My heart grew sick on account of the dampness of the catacombs. I hastened to make an end of my labour. I forced the last stone into its position; I plastered it up. Against the new masonry I re-erected the old rampart of bones. For the half of a century no mortal has disturbed them. *In pace requiescat!*

THE SQUAW

Bram Stoker

Nurnberg at the time was not so much exploited as it has been since then. Irving had not been playing *Faust*, and the very name of the old town was hardly known to the great bulk of the travelling public. My wife and I being in the second week of our honeymoon naturally wanted someone else to join our party, so that when the cheery stranger, Elias P. Hutcheson, hailing from Isthmian City, Bleeding Gulch, Maple Tree County, Neh., turned up at the station at Frankfort, and casually remarked that he was going on to see the most all-fired old Methusaleh of a town in Yurrup, and that he guessed that so much travelling alone was enough to send an intelligent, active citizen into the melancholy ward of a daft house, we took the pretty broad hint and suggested that we should join forces. We found, on comparing notes afterwards, that we had each intended to speak with some diffidence or hesitation so as not to appear too eager, such not being a good compliment to the success of our married life; but the effect was entirely marred by both of us beginning to speak at the same instant—stopping simultaneously and then going on together again. Anyhow, no matter how, it was done; and Elias P. Hutcheson became one of our party. Straightaway Amelia and I found the pleasant benefit; instead of quarrelling, as we had been doing, we found that the restraining influence of a third party was such that we now took every opportunity of spooning in odd corners. Amelia declares that ever since she has, as a result of that experience, advised all her friends to take a friend on the honeymoon. Well, we 'did' Nurnberg together, and much enjoyed the racy remarks of our Transatlantic friend, who, from his quaint speech and his wonderful stock of adventures, might have stepped out of a novel. We kept for the last object of interest in the city to be visited, the Burg, and on the day appointed for the visit strolled round the outer wall of the city by the eastern side.

The Burg is seated on a rock dominating the town, and an immensely deep fosse guards it on the northern side. Nurnberg has been happy in that it was never sacked; had it been it would certainly not be so spick and span perfect as it is at present. The ditch has not been used for centuries, and now its base is spread with tea—gardens and orchards, of which some of the trees are of quite respectable growth. As we wandered round the wall, dawdling in the hot July sunshine, we often paused to admire the views spread before us, and in especial the great plain covered with towns and villages and bounded with a blue line of hills, like a landscape of Claude Lorraine. From this we always turned with new delight to the city itself, with its myriad of quaint old gables and acre-wide red roofs dotted with dormer windows, tier upon tier. A little to our right rose the towers of the Burg, and nearer still, standing grim, the Torture Tower, which was, and is, perhaps, the most interesting place in the city. For centuries the tradition of the Iron Virgin of Nurnberg has been handed down as an instance of the horrors of cruelty of which man is capable; we had long looked forward to seeing it; and here at last was its home.

In one of our pauses we leaned over the wall of the moat and looked down. The garden seemed quite fifty or sixty feet below us, and the sun pouring into it with an intense, moveless heat like that of an oven. Beyond rose the grey, grim wall seemingly of endless height, and losing itself right and left in the angles of bastion and counterscarp. Trees and bushes crowned the wall, and above again towered the lofty houses on whose massive beauty Time has only set the hand of approval. The sun was hot and we were lazy; time was our own, and we lingered, leaning on the wall. Just below us was a pretty sight—a great black cat lying stretched in the sun, whilst round her gambolled prettily a tiny black kitten. The mother would wave her tail for the kitten to play with, or would raise her feet and push away the little one as an encouragement to further play. They were just at the foot of the wall, and Elias P. Hutcheson, in order to help the play, stooped and took from the walk a moderate-sized pebble.

'See!' he said, 'I will drop it near the kitten, and they will both wonder where it came from.'

'Oh, be careful,' said my wife; 'you might hit the dear little thing!'

'Not me, ma'am,' said Elias P. 'Why, I'm as tender as a Maine cherry tree. Lor, bless ye, I wouldn't hurt the poor pooty little critter more'n I'd scalp a baby. An' you may bet your variegated socks on that! See, I'll drop it fur away on the outside so's not to go near her!' Thus saying, he leaned over and held his arm out at full length and dropped the stone. It may be that there is some attractive force which draws lesser matters to greater; or more probably that the wall was not plumb but sloped to its base—we not noticing the inclination from above; but the stone fell with a sickening thud that came up to us through the hot air, right on the kitten's head, and shattered out its little brains then and there. The black cat cast a swift upward glance, and we saw her eyes like green fire fixed an instant on Elias P. Hutcheson; and then her attention was given to the kitten, which lay still with just a quiver other tiny limbs, whilst a thin red stream trickled from a gaping wound. With a muffled cry, such as a human being might give, she bent over the kitten licking its wound and moaning. Suddenly she seemed to realize that it was dead, and again threw her eyes up at us. I shall never forget the sight, for she looked the perfect incarnation of hate. Her green eyes blazed with lurid fire, and the white, sharp teeth seemed to almost shine through the blood which dabbled her mouth and whiskers. She gnashed her teeth, and her claws stood out stark and at full length on every paw. Then she made a wild rush up the wall as if to reach us, but when the momentum ended fell back and further added to her horrible appearance, for she fell on the kitten and rose with her black fur smeared with its brains and blood. Amelia turned quite faint, and I had to lift her back from the wall. There was a seat close by in shade of a spreading plane tree, and here I placed her whilst she composed herself Then I went back to Hutcheson, who stood without moving, looking down on the angry cat below.

As I joined him, he said:

'Wall, I guess that air the savagest beast I ever see—'cept once when an Apache squaw had an edge on a half-breed what they nicknamed "Splinters" 'cos of the way he fixed up heripapoose which he stole on a raid just to show that he appreciated the way they had given his mother the fire torture. She got that kinder look so set on her face that it jest seemed to grow there. She followed Splinters more'n three year till at last the braves got him and handed him over to her. They did say that no man, white or Injun, had ever been so long a-dying under the tortures of the Apaches. The only time I ever see her smile was when I wiped her out. I kem on the camp just in time to see Splinters pass in his checks, and he wasn't sorry to go either. He was a hard citizen, and though I never could shake with him after that papoose business'—for it was bitter bad, and he should have been a white man, for he looked like one—I see he had got paid out in full. Durn me, but I took a piece of his hide from one of his skinnin' posts an' had it made into a pocket-book. It's here now!' and he slapped the breast pocket of his coast.

Whilst he was speaking, the cat was continuing her frantic efforts to get up the wall. She would take a run back and then charge up, sometimes reaching an incredible height. She did not seem to mind the heavy fall which she got each time but started with renewed vigour; and at every tumble her appearance became more horrible. Hutcheson was a kind-hearted man—my wife and I had both noticed little acts of kindness to animals as well as to persons—and he seemed concerned at the state of fury to which the cat had wrought herself.

'Wall, now!' he said, 'I du declare that that poor critter seems quite desperate. There! there! poor thing, it was all an accident—though that won't bring back your little one to you. Say! I wouldn't have had such a thing happen for a thousand! Just shows what a clumsy fool of a man can do when he tries to play! Seems I'm too darned slipper-handed to even play with a cat. Say, Colonell'—it was a pleasant way he had to bestow titles freely—'I hope your wife don't hold no grudge against me on account of this unpleasantness. Why, I wouldn't have had it occur on no account.'

He came over to Amelia and apologized profusely, and she

with her usual kindness of heart hastened to assure him that she quite understood that it was an accident. Then we all went again to the wall and looked over.

The cat missing Hutcheson's face had drawn back across the moat, and was sitting on her haunches as though ready to spring. Indeed, the very instant she saw him she did spring, and with a blind, unreasoning fury, which would have been grotesque, only that it was so frightfully real. She did not try to run up the wall, but simply launched herself at him as though hate and fury could lend her wings to pass straight through the great distance between them. Amelia, womanlike, got quite concerned and said to Elias P. in a warning voice:

'Oh! you must be very careful. That animal would try to kill you if she were here; her eyes look like positive murder.'

He laughed out jovially. 'Excuse me, ma'am,' he said, 'but I "can't help laughin'. Fancy a man that has fought grizzlies an' Injuns bein' careful of bein' murdered by a cat!'

When the cat heard him laugh, her whole demeanour seemed to change. She no longer tried to jump or run up the wall, but went quietly over, and sitting again beside the dead kitten, began to lick and fondle it as though it were alive.

'See!' said I, 'the effect of a really strong man. Even that animal in the midst other fury recognises the voice of a master, and bows to him!'

'Like a squaw!' was the only comment of Elias P. Hutcheson, as we moved on our way round the city fosse. Every now and then we looked over the wall and each time saw the cat following us. At first she had kept going back to the dead kitten, and then as the distance grew greater, she took it in her mouth and so followed. After a while, however, she abandoned this, for we saw her following all alone; she had evidently hidden the body somewhere. Amelia's alarm grew at the cat's persistence, and more than once she repeated her warning; but the American always laughed with amusement, till finally, seeing that she was beginning to be worried, he said:

'I say, ma'am, you needn't be skcered over that cat. I go heeled, I du!' Here he slapped his pistol pocket at the back of his lumbar region. 'Why, sooner'n have you worried, I'll shoot the critter, right here, an' risk the police interferin' with a citizen of the United States for carryin' arms contrairy to regulations!' As he spoke he looked over the wall, but the cat, on seeing him, retreated with a growl into a bed of tall flowers and was hidden. He went on: 'Blest if that ar critter ain't got more sense of what's good for her than most Christians. I guess we've seen the last of her! You bet, she'll go back now to that busted kitten and have a private funeral of it, all to herself!'

Amelia did not like to say more, lest he might, in mistaken kindness to her, fulfil his threat of shooting the cat: and so we went on and crossed the little wooden bridge leading to the gateway whence ran the steep paved roadway between the Burg and the pentagonal Torture Tower. As we crossed the bridge we saw the cat again down below us. When she saw us, her fury seemed to return and she made frantic efforts to get up the steep wall. Hutcheson laughed as he looked down at her, and said:

'Goodbye, old girl. Sorry I injured your feelin's, but you'll get over it in time! So long!' And then we passed through the long, dim archway and came to the gate of the Burg.

When we came out again after our survey of this most beautiful old place which not even the well-intentioned efforts of the Gothic restorers of forty years ago have been able to spoil—though their restoration was then glaring white—we seemed to have quite forgotten the unpleasant episode of the morning. The old lime tree with its great trunk gnarled with the passing of nearly nine centuries, the deep well cut through the heart of the rock by those captives of old, and the lovely view from the city wall whence we heard, spread over almost a full quarter of an hour, the multitudinous chimes of the city, had all helped to wipe out from our minds the incident of the slain kitten.

We were the only visitors who had entered the Torture Tower that morning—so at least said the old custodian—and as we had the place all to ourselves were able to make a minute and more satisfactory survey than would have otherwise been possible. The custodian, looking to us as the sole source of his gains for the day, was willing to meet our wishes in any way. The Torture Tower is truly a grim place, even now when many thousands of visitors have sent a stream of life, and the joy that follows life, into the place; but at the time I mention, it wore its grimmest and most gruesome aspect. The dust of ages seemed to have settled on it, and the darkness and the horror of its memories seem to have become sentient in a way that would have satisfied the Pantheistic souls of Philo or Spinoza. The lower chamber, where we entered, was seemingly, in its normal state, filled with incarnate darkness; even the hot sunlight streaming in through the door seemed to be lost in the vast thickness of the walls, and only showed the masonry rough as when the builder's scaffolding had come down, but coated with dust and marked here and there with patches of dark stain which, if walls could speak, could have given their own dread memories of fear and pain. We were glad to pass up the dusty wooden staircase, the custodian leaving the outer door open to light us somewhat on our way; for to our eyes the one long-wick'd, evil-smelling candle stuck in a sconce on the wall gave an inadequate light. When we came up through the open trap in the corner of the chamber overhead, Amelia held on to me so tightly that I could actually feel her heart beat. I must say for my own part that I was not surprised at her fear, for this room was even more gruesome than that below. Here there was certainly more light, but only just sufficient to realise the horrible surroundings of the place. The builders of the tower had evidently intended that only they who should gain the top should have any of the joys of light and prospect. There, as we had noticed from below, were ranges of windows, albeit of medieval smallness, but elsewhere in the tower were only a very few narrow slits such as were habitual in places of medieval defence. A few of these only lit the chamber, and these were so high up in the wall that from no part could the sky be seen through the thickness of the walls. In racks, and leaning in disorder against the walls, were a number of headsmen's swords, great double-handed weapons with broad blade and keen edge. Hard by were several blocks whereon the necks of the victims had lain, with here and there deep notches where the steel had bitten through the guard of flesh and shored into the wood. Round the chamber, placed in all sorts of irregular ways, were many implements of torture which made one's heart ache to see—chairs full of spikes which gave instant and excruciating pain; chairs and couches with dull knobs whose torture was seemingly less, but which, though slower, were equally efficacious; racks, belts, boots, gloves, collars, all made for compressing at will; steel baskets in which the head could be slowly crushed into a pulp if necessary; watchmen's hooks with long handle and knife that cut at resistance—this a specialty of the old Nurnberg police system; and many, many other devices for man's injury to man. Amelia grew quite pale with the horror of things, but fortunately did not faint, for being a little overcome she sat down on a torture chair, but jumped up again with a shriek, all tendency to faint gone. We both pretended that it was the injury done to her dress by the dust of the chair and the rusty spikes which had upset her, and Mr Hutcheson acquiesced in accepting the explanation with a kind-hearted laugh.

But the central object in the whole of this chamber of horrors was the engine known as the Iron Virgin, which stood near the centre of the room. It was a rudely-shaped figure of a woman, something of the bell order, or, to make a closer comparison, of the figure of Mrs Noah in the children's Ark, but without that slimness of waist and perfect *rondeur* of hip which marks the aesthetic type of the Noah family One would hardly have recognized it as intended for a human figure at all had not the founder shaped on the forehead a rude semblance of a woman's face. This machine was coated with rust without, and covered with dust; a rope was fastened to a ring in the front of the figure, about where the waist should have been, and was drawn through a pulley, fastened on the wooden pillar which sustained the flooring above. The custodian pulling this rope showed that a section of the front was hinged like a door at one side; we then saw that the engine was of considerable thickness, leaving just room enough inside for a man to be placed. The door was of equal thickness and of great weight, for it took the custodian all his strength, aided though he was by the contrivance of the pulley, to open it. This weight was partly due to the fact that the door was of manifest purpose hung so as to throw its weight downwards, so that it might shut of its own accord when the strain was released. The inside was honeycombed with rust—nay more, the rust alone that comes through time would hardly have eaten so deep into the iron walls; the rust of the cruel stains was deep indeed! It was only, however, when we came to look at the inside of the door that the diabolical intention was manifest to the full. Here were several long spikes, square and massive, broad at the base and sharp at the points, placed in such a position that when the door should close, the upper ones would pierce the eyes of the victim and the lower ones his heart and vitals. The sight was too much for poor Amelia, and this time she fainted dead off, and I had to carry her down the stairs and place her on a bench outside till she recovered. That she felt it to the quick was afterwards shown by the fact that my eldest son bears to this day a rude birthmark on his breast, which has, by family consent, been accepted as representing the Nurnberg Virgin.

When we got back to the chamber, we found Hutcheson still opposite the Iron Virgin; he had been evidently philosophizing, and now gave us the benefits of this thought in the shape of a sort of exordium.

'Wall, I guess I've been learnin' somethin' here while madam has been getting over her faint. 'Pears to me that we're a long way behind the times on our side of the big drink. We uster think out on the plains that the Injun could give us points in tryin' to make a man on comfortable; but I guess your old medieval law-and-order party could raise him every time. Splinters was pretty good in his bluff on the squaw, but this here young miss held a straight flush all high on him. The points of them spikes air sharp enough still, though even the edges air eaten out by what uster be on them. It'd be a god thing for our Indian section to get some specimens of this here play-toy to send round to the Reservations jest to knock the stuffin' out of the bucks, and the squaws too, by showing them as how old civilization lays over them at their best. Guess but I'll get in that box a minute jest to see how it feels!'

'Oh no! no!!' said Amelia. 'It is too terrible!'

'Guess, ma'am, nothin's too terrible to the explorin' mind. I've been in some queer places in my time. Spent a night inside a dead horse while a prairie fire swept over me in Montana Territory—an' another time slept inside a dead buffler when the Comanches was on the war path an' didn't keer to leave my kyard on them. I've been two days in a caved-in tunnel in the Billy Broncho gold mine in New Mexico an' was one of the four shut up for three parts of a day in the caisson what slid over on her side when we was settin' the foundations of the Buffalo Bridge. I've not funked an odd experience yet, an' I don't propose to begin now!'

We saw that he was set on the experiment, so I said: 'Well, hurry up, old man, and get through it quick!'

'All right, General,' said he, 'but I calculate we ain't quite ready yet. The gentlemen, my predecessors, what stood in that thar canister, didn't volunteer for the office—not much! And I guess there was some ornamental tyin' up before the big stroke was made. I want to go into this thing fair and square, so I must get fixed up proper first. I dare say this old galoot can rise some string and tie me up accordin' to sample?'

This was said interrogatively to the old custodian, but the latter, who understood the drift of his speech, though perhaps not appreciating to the full the niceties of dialect and imagery, shook his head. His protest was, however, only formal and made to be overcome. The American thrust a gold piece into his hand, saying, 'Take it, pard! it's your pot; and don't be skcer'd. This ain't no necktie party that you're asked to assist in!' He produced some thin frayed rope and proceeded to bind our companion with sufficient strictness for the purpose. When the upper part of his body was bound, Hutcheson said:

'Hold on a moment, Judge. Guess I'm too heavy for you to tote into the canister. You jest let me walk in, and then you can wash up regardin' my legs!'

Whilst speaking he had backed himself into the opening which was just enough to hold him. It was a close fit and no mistake. Amelia looked on with fear in her eyes, but she evidently did not like to say anything. Then the custodian completed his task by tying the American's feet together so that he was now absolutely helpless and fixed in his voluntary prison. He seemed to really enjoy it, and the incipient smile which was habitual to his face blossomed into actuality as he said:

'Guess this here Eve was made out of the rib of a dwarf! There ain't much room for a full-grown citizen of the United States to hustle. We uster make our coffins more roomier in Idaho territory. Now, Judge, you jest begin to let this door down, slow, on to me. I want to feel the same pleasure as the other jays had when those spikes began to move toward their eyes!'

'Oh no! no! no!' broke in Amelia hysterically. 'It is too terrible! I can't bear to see it!—I can't I can't!'

But the American was obdurate. 'Say, Colonel,' said he, 'why not take Madame for a little promenade? I wouldn't hurt her feelin's for the world; but now that I am here, havin' kem eight thousand miles, wouldn't it be too hard to give up the very experience I've been pinin' an' pantin' fur? A man can't get to feel like canned goods every time! Me and the Judge here'll fix up this thing in no time, an' then you'll come back, an' we'll all laugh together!'

Once more the resolution that is born of curiosity

triumphed, and Amelia stayed holding tight to my arm and shivering whilst the custodian began to slacken slowly inch by inch the rope that held back the iron door. Hutcheson's face was positively radiant as his eyes followed the first movement of the spikes.

'Wall!' he said, 'I guess I've not had enjoyment like this since I left Noo York. Bar a scrap with a French sailor at Wapping—an' that warn't much of a picnic neither—I've not had a show fur real pleasure in this dod-rotted Continent, where there ain't no b'ars nor no Injuns, an' wheer nary man goes heeled. Slow there, Judge! Don't you rush this business! I want a show for my money this game—I du!'

The custodian must have had in him some of the blood of his predecessors in that ghastly tower, for he worked the engine with a deliberate and excruciating slowness which after five minutes, in which the outer edge of the door had not moved half as many inches, began to overcome Amelia. I saw her lips whiten, and felt her hold upon my arm relax. I looked around an instant for a place whereon to lay her, and when I looked at her again found that her eye had become fixed on the side of the Virgin. Following its direction I saw the black cat crouching out of sight. Her green eyes shone like danger lamps in the gloom of the place, and their colour was heightened by the blood which still smeared her coat and reddened her mouth. I cried out:

'The cat! look out for the cat!' for even then she sprang out before the engine. At this moment she looked like a triumphant demon. Her eyes blazed with ferocity, her hair bristled out till she seemed twice her normal size, and her tail lashed about as does a tiger's when the quarry is before it. Elias P. Hutcheson when he saw her was amused, and his eyes positively sparkled with fun as he said:

'Darned if the squaw hain't got on all her war paint! Jest give her a shove off if she comes any of her tricks on me, for I'm so fixed everlastingly by the boss, that durn my skin if I can keep my eyes from her if she wants them! Easy there, Judge! don't you slack that ar rope or I'm euchered!'

At this moment Amelia completed her faint, and I had to clutch hold of her round the waist or she would have fallen to the floor. Whilst attending to her I saw the black cat crouching for a spring, and jumped up to turn the creature out.

But at that instant, with a sort of hellish scream, she hurled herself, not as we expected at Hutcheson, but straight at the face of the custodian. Her claws seemed to be tearing wildly as one sees in the Chinese drawings of the dragon rampant, and as I looked

I saw one of them light on the poor man's eye and actually tear through it and down his cheek, leaving a wide band of red where the blood seemed to spurt from every vein.

With a yell of sheer terror which came quicker than even his sense of pain, the man leaped back, dropping as he did so the rope which held back the iron door. I jumped for it, but was too late, for the cord ran like lightning through the pulley-block, and the heavy mass fell forward from its own weight.

As the door closed I caught a glimpse of our poor companion's face. He seemed frozen with terror. His eyes stared with a horrible anguish, as if dazed, and no sound came from his lips.

And then the spikes did their work. Happily the end was quick, for when I wrenched open the door they had pierced so deep that they had locked in the bones of the skull through which they had crushed, and actually tore him—it—out of his iron prison till, bound as he was, he fell at full length with a sickly thud upon the floor, the face turning upward as he fell.

I rushed to my wife, lifted her up and carried her out, for I feared For her very reason if she should wake from her faint to such a scene. I laid her on the bench outside and ran back. Leaning against the wooden column was the custodian moaning in pain whilst he held his reddening handkerchief to his eyes. And sitting on the head of the poor American was the cat, purring loudly as she licked the blood which trickled through the gashed socket of his eyes.

I think no one will call me cruel because I seized one of the old executioner's swords and shore her in two as she sat.